DANCE JAM PRODUCTIONS

Celise Downs

BookLocker.com, Inc.
2009

Cover images: istockphoto.com/draco77(cover illustration); AYokovlev(girl dancer silhouette)

For Michael John Coppinger
I told you I would write about it someday.

CHAPTER ONE

The Announcement

A phone rang incessantly over the throbbing beat of Michael Jackson's "Smooth Criminal." Head bobbing, hips swaying, fingers snapping, Mataya Black Hawk picked up the receiver on the fourth ring.

"Rhythm Station, how may I help you?"

"I hope you're sitting down," the caller responded.

Mataya rolled her eyes at her best friend's version of hello. More often than not, Renee Hathaway's conversations started with that phrase, and usually amounted to nothing more than dramatic exaggeration.

"Ren, I work at a dance studio. I'm *never* sitting down," Mataya remarked dryly.

"You are *so* right, Mattie. So I take it you haven't heard the news."

Mattie stopped dancing, her fingers stalled in mid-snap. "What news?" she asked warily.

"About DJP," Ren said.

Mattie's heart sped up as all sorts of possibilities raced through her mind. *Dance Jam Productions* was the most popular show for teenagers since *MTV*. Produced right here in Phoenix, it was an hour-long dance party with music videos, movie reviews, and the latest music news. On Friday and Saturday nights, seventeen to twenty-year-olds could head down to Club Avatar, the under twenty-one nightclub, dance till one am, and be filmed the whole time. If you were lucky, you'd see yourself on television some time during the week.

Mattie and her friends had gone every weekend and had danced till their feet hurt. Then Ren's work schedule had changed, much to her dismay, so now they only occasionally hit the club. The coveted position of being a regular had been given to the best dancers. And even then, they had to audition for it. The coolest part about her job was that she got to see those dancers every day after school since they practiced at Rhythm Station.

"You there? Anybody home? You better not have zoned out on me, Mattie."

Ren's indignant tone brought her attention back around.

"I'm here, Ren, I'm here. What news are you talking about?" Mattie instinctively steeled herself for the worst. Were they canceling the show? Getting new hosts?

"Dance contest. Tomorrow afternoon," Ren announced.

Mattie backed up to a chair and numbly dropped into it, her mouth sagging in stunned shock. "A-are you saying what I think you're saying?" she whispered.

There was a short pause. "What am I saying?" Ren deadpanned, then ruined the whole effect by laughing. "Isn't it crash, Mattie? *Dance Jam* is looking for more regular dancers. There's gonna be a dance contest tomorrow at Sun Devil Stadium. Twelve finalists are gonna be chosen to participate in a dance-off next Friday at the club. After that, they're gonna narrow it down to six, who will get to dance again on Saturday. And here's the kicker, Mattie. The show's being syndicated. DJP is going *national*, baby. Can you believe it? This is *so* totally crash," she babbled excitedly. "So what's the plan?"

Mattie's head was spinning from the news, so Ren's question went by the wayside for a moment. "How'd you find out about the contest?" she asked.

Ren's exasperated sigh reached through the phone lines and practically blew the hair off Mattie's forehead. "Hel-*lo*, like, they've been talking about it all week on the show. Haven't you been watching?" she questioned.

"Well, seeing as how I go to school during the day and work here until six—"

"But you tape it, Mattie. Religiously," Ren interjected.

She's got me there, Mattie thought. Instead of taping soap operas, she taped *Dance Jam Productions.*

"Mattie? Mataya, are you there?" Ren yelled into the phone.

"Yeah, yeah, I'm here," she answered.

"Mattie, what's going on with you? You're hardly ever home at night anymore. Mici and I call you all the time, but you're never home."

"I've been staying late here at the studio," Mattie told her.

"Oh, I should've known. You get to use the studio after hours, huh? That's cool. Are y'all havin' another dance concert?" she asked.

"Yeah. Some time next month, I think," Mattie returned absently. "I've been working on a few new steps."

"I'm surprised you weren't the one telling *me.* About the contest, I mean. The dancers are still there, aren't they?" Ren wanted to know.

Without thinking, Mattie turned her head towards the huge double doors to her left. One of the doors was slightly ajar and the sounds of clapping hands, stomping feet, and throbbing music could be heard.

"Yeah, they're still here," she confirmed.

"They never mentioned anything to you?"

"By the time I get here, they're already practicing. Besides, they come here to dance, not socialize," Mattie said, her right foot tapping to the beat of the music.

"Well, yeah, but still. They see you every day. Ever since *Dance Jam* came here and they chose your studio to rehearse at, they've seen you. I *know* they don't ignore you when they see you. They haven't said a word to you?" she asked.

Mattie and rolled her eyes again. "Maybe they aren't allowed to, Ren, did you ever think of that? It's probably against the rules or something," she pointed out.

"Oh. I never thought of that," Ren said in a low tone. "Well, maybe Mici and I can come over later and we can work on something."

"That would be cool. I might stay after for an hour or two, so I'll call you when I get home," Mattie said.

"Ty workin' late again tonight?" Ren inquired.

"Yep." Mattie didn't bother to elaborate.

"He still picks you up from work?"

Mattie leaned back in her chair. "Sometimes," she answered quietly.

"The man sure likes to keep tabs on you. Don't you think he's taking the legal guardian thing a bit too seriously?"

Mattie's breath came out in a blustery sigh as she rubbed her fingers across her forehead. "Ren, there are certain things you don't understand about Ty and his culture. He's very protective," she said.

Mattie tried to convince herself that it wasn't a complete lie. Her best friends just thought that Tykota had worked for a company that specialized in security systems and personal protection. Of course, those weren't the only services they offered, but her friends didn't need to know *everything.* Being cautious and maintaining her privacy were lessons she had been taught at a young age. *And like the saying goes, old habits die hard. Or they just die.*

"…Don't understand, even after all these years, but still…" Ren was saying.

"Look, I don't stay late all the time. Lately, he just follows me home. You know I drive every chance I get. I feel like I'm your personal freakin' chauffeur sometimes. As if you don't have your *own* car," Mattie teased, trying to lighten the mood as well as change the subject.

"I don't need a car. I've got my board," her friend quipped.

Mattie chuckled. Ren was a Louisiana-born skater chick at heart, right down to the baggy pants and wallet chain that dangles halfway down the pant-leg. "Don't worry. Everything's fine. Listen, I know you're not on break over there, and it'll be getting busy here soon, so I'd better go."

"Me, too. I think I see some punk tryin' to make off with some elbow pads. Call me later?"

Mattie shook her head. Ren's job at Thrash Town, a store that sold skate gear to Tony Hawk wannabes, was right up her alley. Mattie definitely wouldn't want to be that guy with the elbow pads.

"Yeah. I'll call you," she assured her friend.

"Don't forget to watch today's episode," Ren reminded her. "They're going to announce it again, I just know it."

"Okay," Mattie replied.

"And tell Chris I said *hi*."

Ren said the word in such a breathy tone that Mattie burst out laughing. Chris Morrow was a regular on *Dance Jam*. He was also the unknowing object of a crush that had begun the minute Ren had seen him on TV almost eight months ago. Getting a chance to meet him, let alone dance with him every day, was incentive enough for her to sign up for the contest.

"I'll tell him," Mattie said.

"I'd better go. That kid looks guilty. Catch ya later, Mattie," she said.

"Bye." Mattie barely got the word out before the dial tone hummed in her ear.

Forty-five minutes and four phone calls later, she got up, stretched, then stood in the doorway, absently tapping her foot to the beat, as she watched the dancers work through a difficult step. After a few minutes, she pushed away, closed the door, and strolled back to the desk, her thoughts turning to the dance contest. So *Dance Jam* was looking for more dancers. *Wouldn't it be a hoot if I actually got chosen?* Ren thought that just because Mattie knew the dancers, she would be an automatic shoo-in.

That probably wasn't far from the truth, now that she thought about it. She knew their dance routines, especially the ones they always performed at the beginning and at the end of the show, and she definitely knew their music. Music had been a constant entity in her life ever since Tykota had reappeared ten years ago.

Glancing at one of the two framed pictures on her desk, Mattie reached for it. At six foot four and thirty-two years of age, Tykota Black Hawk was a powerfully built man of Native American descent. His voice was a deep and soothing resonant sound that washed over her like a healing rain and had lulled her to sleep when she was little. The words had not made sense at first, for he sang in his native tongue, but that had never mattered to her. His voice had kept the nightmares at bay. And later, his songs had made her forget the horror she'd not only witnessed but also had been a victim of herself.

Tykota sang to her only on special occasions now, but the music remained a necessity. Her personal tastes leaned towards alternative and New Age. The music selection at Rhythm Station ran the full gamut from Celtic to R and B.

She set the picture of Tykota back and shifted her gaze to the one next to her computer. Dressed in floor-length silk gowns, high heels, and costume jewelry, Mattie and her two best friends had struck poses a la En Vogue for Tykota's photographer's eye. Mattie smiled, remembering her sophomore year at Catalina Valley High, sixth period dance class. She had been paired up with Ren and Michelle Fontenot as part of a class project. After talking for a few minutes, they realized they had one major thing in common: *Dance Jam Productions.*

Mattie was amazed she'd fit in with them so well. At five foot seven, Ren's close-cropped, burnished gold hair framed a round pixie face. Long brown lashes accented dark green eyes that sparkled with inner mischief, and a light sprinkling of freckles graced a nose that could only be described as "button cute." She carried her skateboard around like an additional limb, but the picture on Mattie's desk was proof that Ren was a female first and a skater second.

Willowy and graceful at five-eight, Mici (pronounced Mickey) had a short cap of fiery red hair, parted deeply on the left side and cut high in the back so the sides angled down. Eyes the color of aged whiskey peered from a freckle-free porcelain-smooth face. Black half glasses that Ren had deemed "beatnik" perched atop a lean nose. Everyone said Mici should be a model, but her response was always "*Cherie,* I'll draw up a star chart for a model, but I'd never want to *be* a model. I'm not really into haute couture." Maybe being born in Paris, France, fashion capitol of the world, tended to desensitize a person from all the glamour. Despite the fact that she'd been living in the States since she was six, Mici liked to keep her roots afloat by using French words on occasion.

Then there was Mattie. At five foot five, she considered herself a duck among swans. Her wavy, dark brown hair stopped short of her waist. A small, tip-tilted nose hovered above a full mouth in a gently rounded olive-toned face. Reaching up, she passed a finger under her right eye. Her almond-shaped eyes had been brown once. A deep, coffee bean brown, if she remembered right. Now, unusually pale blue orbs stared back at her every morning in the mirror; a pallid ice color that seemed unnatural on a person whose skin was so dark. She had nothing to compare them to, for she herself had never seen anyone with eyes of so pale a color. If *she* couldn't think of anything nice to say, what made her think any potential male suitors could come up with something?

Yet Ren had found something. "My brother used to have a big marble that same color. His shooter, I think. I'm pretty sure he still carries it around in his pocket. Like a good luck charm, y'know?"

Mici had been pretty encouraging, too. "I *know* I had a crystal that color, *cherie*. Great for channeling."

And Tykota had been very poetic. "They remind me of the glaciers in Alaska. When it's just nothing but water and ice for miles and miles."

Mattie sighed and crossed her arms over chest, wishing her own quirks were as simple as sparkling apple juice (Ren's favorite) and mood bracelets (Mici's jewelry of choice). Hers were more deep-rooted, necessitating body coverage from breastbone to waist. No half shirts, tank tops, or bikini tops for her. She had too many secrets to hide, physically and mentally. But then she'd found *Dance Jam Productions*. The music that had followed her throughout her life finally had an outlet. She'd perfected her dance skills by watching her friends and the *DJP* dancers.

Mattie turned her head and scrutinized the studio, blessing the day she had come to have the perfect job of being Rhythm Station's receptionist. Located in a small strip mall off Bell Road, it looked like a typical dance studio. Framed posters of *A Chorus Line*, *Cats*, *Fame*, and *West Side Story* shared wall space with pictures of Baryshnikov, Nureyev, and the Alvin Ailey Dance Troupe. The combined color scheme of black, fire engine red, and sunshine yellow reflected both the owner and the feeling of dance-fun and energy.

Rhythm Station offered Modern Jazz, Ballet, Tap, Hip-Hip, Ballroom, and Highland dancing for all ages at all levels. Dance concerts were held twice a year, and in-studio concerts once a month; some students entered nationwide competitions. Mattie learned something new every day about the owner, the company, and the business of dance in general. The job also gave her the opportunity to become privy to all the latest gossip about *Dance Jam Productions*. Such as the upcoming dance contest, for instance. News of *DJP* traveled to her without fail, so she was bugged that this latest tidbit had bypassed her ears. She'd never expected the show to need dancers after being on the air for only two years. Who would want to leave, anyway? All the regulars looked so professional they'd probably worn leotards as babies instead of diapers.

Mattie walked back to her desk, fingering the band of white jade surrounding her right thumb. What would it be like to dance on national television? She didn't have a problem performing in front an auditorium full of people. A panel of judges didn't cause panic attacks, either. National television, however, was a different bag of Cheetos. The double doors were flung open and the object of Ren's affections strode out, interrupting her thoughts.

"Hey, beautiful, how's it goin'?" Chris Morrow greeted with a flirtatious smile.

A smile that flashed lady-killer in blinking red neon lights, Mattie thought.

"Good, Chris. You guys done for the day?" she inquired, rounding the desk to sit down.

"Yep. You're gonna come down to the park tomorrow, right?" he asked.

"I'm not sure yet," she admitted truthfully.

Chris began to walk backwards as the other dancers spilled into the lobby. He was almost out the door when he said, "Oh, and bring someone with you. Preferably one of the opposite sex.

Unless you know of a female who can do lifts." With a cheeky smile and a waggle of eyebrows, Chris was gone.

Mattie's breath escaped her chest as though she'd been squeezed. A partner. Okay, *that* was something she obviously hadn't thought through very well. It was to be expected, of course. All the regular dancers had partners and the Dance Showcase was an important segment of the program. Yet the idea of close contact with the opposite sex brought up memories she never wanted to relive again. She could handle familial hugs from Ty and his best friends. But dancing up close and personal with someone she didn't know was different. *Maybe I could get out if it somehow,* Mattie thought. *Maybe I could fake a sprain right before—*

The shrill ring of the telephone made Mattie jump. "Rhythm Station, how may I help you?" she took a short calming breath.

"Hello, my island beauty." A familiar smooth, deep voice flowed through the wires.

"Hello, guardian of my heart." Mattie slipped easily into the language Tykota had taught her as a young girl.

He called her every day at work and the exchange was always the same, always in his native tongue. It was a language she had learned during her first year with him, and that was how all their phone conversations were conducted. It was a tactic that was useful in his line of business, for the members of his special unit were fluent in his language.

"How are things going over there?" he asked.

She hesitated for a fraction of a second, hoping Tykota wouldn't notice. "Good."

"I will probe later, but there is something I want to tell you," he said.

"Good news, I hope."

Mattie could hear the smile in his voice as he said, "Yes, it is good news. Kedren and Skylar are getting married."

Mattie gasped in delight. She had met Kedren Price and his friends and had grown close to them during the time their parents had been employees of Zion Security. When all of their parents had been killed in a plane crash, and it was discovered the crash hadn't been accidental, Kedren and his friends had become temporary employees of Zion Security and Mattie had lost touch with them. At the age of seventeen, Kedren had solved his parents' murder and had fallen in love with Skylar Knight. The scandal surrounding that assignment had rocked Skylar's high school four years ago, and people were still talking about it to this day.

"Oh, Ty, that's wonderful. When's the happy day?"

"Sometime next year. They do not have a set date yet, but knowing Skylar, they should have one soon," Tykota replied. "I hear discontent in your voice, sweetling. I thought you liked that job?"

Geez, beat around the bush why don't you? Mattie thought wryly. "I love this job. I was just debating on what I should do," she said aloud.

"What you should do about what?"

"*Dance Jam Productions* is having a dance contest tomorrow afternoon with a big dance-off next Saturday. The show is looking for another pair of regular dancers and I'm just wondering if I should go. I mean, Ren is totally psyched about this whole thing..." she trailed off.

"But you are not," he guessed.

"I was at first. I mean, I love to dance. *DJP* is my favorite show and I think it would be so much fun, even if I didn't get to be a finalist, but there has to be two people. As in boy and girl."

For a few moments Mattie heard nothing but the faint buzzing of wires. Then Ty intoned solemnly, "People only know what you tell them." After another short pause he continued, "Are you staying late today?"

"Yeah. 'Til six-thirty," she informed him.

"All right. I will come for you at six-thirty."

"Okay. See you then."

Hanging up, Mattie stared unseeingly out the front doors. *People only know what you tell them.* Instinctively, she passed a hand down the front of her T-shirt, coming to rest at her stomach. She'd kept her secret since she was seven years old. *People only know what you tell them.* No one was going to know, she assured herself. Because she was never going to tell.

CHAPTER TWO

Mattie Meets Jarek

At that moment, the phone rang and a customer stepped in simultaneously. Jerking her thoughts back to the present, Mattie hurriedly put her headphones on and answered the call. Once finished, she punched the button to disconnect the call. Then she looked up. And swallowed with difficulty.

"Good afternoon. May I help you?" she asked in a strangled tone."I'm here to see Liz," teenage guy said with a friendly smile.

Mattie blindly reached up to make sure the microphone was close enough to her mouth.

"She just finished a class, and you are...?"

"Jarek," he supplied.

She nodded once and punched a button. *Why does that name sound so familiar?*

"Liz? Jarek is here to see you," she announced, then paused to listen. "Okay. No problem. You're welcome."

Mattie looked up at the guy with what she hoped was a professional smile. "She said she'd be right out. Why don't you have a seat?" she suggested.

Jarek nodded and Mattie cleared her throat.

"Okay."

Turning, he headed for the couch and sat down, picking up a magazine as he did so. Mattie gave him a sweeping glance before returning her attention to the message pad in front of her. The observation had been swift, but she'd been able to catalogue everything about him. Doc Marten boots, slightly baggy Guess jeans, and a white tank top molded a perfectly muscled physique. *Baseball*, she thought, *possibly soccer*. Hair as black and straight as Tykota's stopped just short of his shoulders.

His face was just as unforgettable. A mischievous grin that started on one side of his mouth revealed straight, white teeth when the grin became a full-blown smile. Black eyebrows arched over green eyes that reminded Mattie of the waters of Maui, and his chiseled jawbone was reminiscent of a young Pierce Brosnan. The gorgeous gene was definitely swimming around in his genetic pool. He ran a casual hand through his hair, making Mattie wonder if it was as soft as it appeared. Out of the corner of her eye, she watched as he slouched down on the couch and stretched his legs out before him. Sliding a section of hair behind one ear, he lazily flipped through the pages of a Dance America magazine. Mattie froze in her chair when he looked over at her for a long moment, before returning to the magazine in his hands.

Mattie's own mouth twisted into a moue at never being able to do something so natural and instinctive as to blatantly stare at someone. Truth be known, she'd really never been able to look at anyone face to face for a certain length of time. At least, not the way she did with her friends. The pale blue eyes that peered like a bright beacon from a dark-skinned face had always made her feel self-conscious and a little freakish. She sensed that people felt uncomfortable looking her in the face, so she'd devised a way in which they wouldn't have to: surreptitious glances and sunglasses.

Suddenly, Liz came bursting through a side door, a huge purse slung over one shoulder.

"And how is my favorite gorgeous nephew?" she crowed, arms wide open.

The nephew. Of course. No wonder the name had rung a bell, Mattie thought. He called Liz about once a week, but she'd never made the connection. She watched as Jarek laughed, tossed the magazine on the table and stood up to embrace the energetic woman.

"Your favorite gorgeous, and *only* nephew, is doing great," he replied in amusement.

"Mattie, you've met Jarek, haven't you?" Liz inquired, slipping an arm around the young man whom stood three inches taller than she did.

"Not formally, no. It's nice to finally match a face to the voice," she said, getting up and walking around the desk.

She instantly felt his gaze scan her body. Today, she had chosen to wear a gray silk ankle-length skirt with a white orchard pattern, and a white ribbed baby T-shirt. Her long wavy hair was pulled up on both sides by seashell combs her mother had made, with one long strand left free to frame her right cheek. Moccasins that Tykota's mother had made for her completed the semi-casual outfit. Unconsciously, she passed her right hand down the side of her skirt before holding it out.

"Mataya Black Hawk," she introduced herself.

"Jarek Thanos. And it's also nice to put a face with the voice. Aunt Liz talks about you all the time," he returned, shaking her proffered hand.

Mattie glanced at Liz, then back to Jarek, who had yet to release her hand. "Does she now? All good, I hope," she said.

"Of course," Jarek riposted.

Mattie took her hand back under the pretense of pushing a strand of hair over her shoulder. Enjoyable though the contact had been, she wasn't used to lingering touches bestowed upon her by a male. Now that she thought about it, Jarek *did* have nicely shaped hands. Perfect for doing lifts.

"Well, we'd better go pick up those bolts of fabric before the warehouse closes," Liz said a bit too loudly. "I have a full afternoon of classes ahead."

CELISE DOWNS

"And I have some business calls to make," Mattie lied smoothly, knowing full well that other businesses usually called *them*.

Jarek nodded, dug out his car keys and propped an expensive pair of sunglasses on his nose.

"It was nice meeting you, Mataya," he said in a soft voice that Mattie could only interpret as flirtatious. She wasn't used to flirtatious. Hell, she didn't even know *how* to flirt.

"Likewise," she replied, flicking him a quick glance.

"Maybe I'll see you again sometime."

Doubt it. "Maybe," she murmured, then turned to Liz. "I'll see you in an hour."

"And not a minute later," Liz said.

Turning on the ball of her foot with a little bounce, Liz shot back over her shoulder, "Hold down the fort, sweetie." Then to Jarek, "So, did you hear about the..."

The closing door cut off the rest of Liz's words. Mattie had a feeling she had mentioned the contest tomorrow. Hands clasped behind her back, she watched them get into a white Nissan Pathfinder with tinted windows and a license plate that read JT JAMS. *Very clever*, she thought. Of course, it was his car because no sane adult would have tires like that on their own car.

But he looked good in it. He'd look good in a Jeep, too A ragtop, maybe, or one with no covering at all. He'd probably look downright smokin' on a motorcycle. The phone rang and she reached out to pick up the headphones. With one last look at the departing vehicle, she slipped on the headphones and pushed a button.

"Good afternoon, Rhythm Station."

***

20

At five-thirty, Liz and Mattie locked the front doors, turned out the lights in the lobby, and went into the studio where Liz taught her classes. Mattie went into the dressing rooms to change, while Liz rifled though the CDs at her music stand. Once dressed, Mattie came out and sat down on the hardwood floor to put on her jazz shoes. She watched Liz sway back and forth to music only she could hear, absently thinking that the woman never stood still. Being the owner of Rhythm Station, and a dance instructor, probably required a lot of energy. Liz Devlin reminded her of a butterfly flitting from petal to leaf. She had a petite Mary Lou Retton figure, and straight jet-black hair that fell just below her ears. Her heart-shaped face housed green eyes the same shade as Jarek's, eyebrows professionally plucked in a "surprise" position, and a pouty mouth that smiled often. This woman was her mentor and her friend, not to mention the most compassionate and patient person she had ever had the fortune to meet.

"He's interested in you." The words bounced around the hollow studio.

Mattie froze for a second before continuing to tie her shoelaces.

"I sensed that," she replied.

"He hardly talked about anything but you while we were loading up on fabric today," Liz said again when Mattie said nothing more. "He wanted to know everything about you."

"Did he now?"

Stretching her legs in front of her, Mattie began to warm up.

"He asked if you had a boyfriend."

"I imagine you told him no." The words were muffled in her lap as she leaned over, but Liz heard them just the same.

"I told him that I didn't know. And I don't. Just because you don't talk about a significant other doesn't mean you don't have one," she pointed out.

"True," Mattie murmured, spreading her legs to stretch to the middle.

"I told him you're a private person who likes to keep her personal life private," Liz added.

"You make it sound like I'm hiding something," Mattie remarked, then immediately wished she could take the words back. *Why on Earth would you say something like* that?

"Are you?" Liz asked.

"Am I what?" she tried to stall.

"Hiding something."

"Would it matter if I was?" Mattie stared a hole in Liz's back until she turned around.

"If it was putting you in danger, yes, it would matter. I'd want to help." Liz returned the stare without blinking.

Mattie nodded. "I have Tykota," she stated.

"Tykota's not female," Liz shot back.

Mattie cocked an eyebrow. "And your point is…?"

"That if you ever need to talk, to a *female,* I'm here for you," Liz said with a shrug.

Mattie gazed at her for a moment longer before saying, "Thanks. I'll be sure to keep that in mind," in a near whisper.

Suddenly, Liz beamed a cheery smile as though the conversation had never turned serious, and turned around to open the CD case.

"So, have you thought about the dance contest?"

Mattie rolled her eyes at the quick subject change, but she was grateful for the reprieve. Her personal life wasn't open for discussion and she tried to head anyone off when the questions became too pointed. Liz, Ren and Mici had learned with a quickness when to back off.

"Some," she replied, stretching to one side.

"You're an excellent dancer, Mattie," Liz pointed out, leaning against the music stand with her arms crossed over her chest.

"I have a good teacher," she drawled with a knowing look.

Liz smiled at the compliment. "You should seriously think about going tomorrow, kiddo. You wouldn't have to worry about a conflict of interest. Anybody can participate except the people affiliated with the show," she relayed.

Mattie blinked twice in confusion. "Then...that would be us."

"Then what would be us?"

Mattie let out a snort of laughter. "Hel-*lo*, get with the program, Liz. *We're* affiliated with the show."

Liz shifted her weight to one leg and put her hands on her hips.

"Girlie, they aren't paying my bills and they sure as hell aren't paying me to choreograph those dance routines. That's Lucy's job. They pay Lucy, she pays me rent space. Therefore, no affiliation," she concluded.

Mattie paused in her exercises to lean back on her hands.

"Really? I didn't know that. About the choreographing and the rent thing, I mean."

"It was before your time, dearie," she retorted in a quivery, old lady voice.

Mattie laughed and shook her head.

"How come you never told me that?"

Liz shrugged again. "You never asked. So what's your next excuse for not going?"

Mattie crossed her legs Indian-style and clasped her hands in her lap. "Why do they need another couple?"

"Someone's leaving."

"Who?"

"Don't know."

"Why?"

"Don't know," Liz shot back.

Mattie's lip twitched in amusement at their rapid verbal exchange.

"So what's the deal with the twelve finalists and the dance-off thing next weekend?"

"Well, it's either The Best or Second Best. The Best become regulars. Second Best get VIP passes. So you get to slide right on through the velvet ropes instead of paying the cover. Simple as that," Liz said with a shoulder shrug.

Mattie nodded, going back to her warm up exercises. At least she'd have more information to tell her friends when they came over tonight. She'd managed a quick phone call to Ren and Mici. Ren had taken the night off and instead of going dancing, they'd decided on a slumber party at Mattie's house.

Liz walked to the music stand and put a CD back in its slot. "Tykota coming for you tonight?"

"Six-thirty," Mattie confirmed.

Liz glanced at her watch. "You got some time left. I'm outta here. Be sure to lock up after yourself," she advised.

"I will," Mattie assured her with a grin.

"Have a good weekend, kiddo."

"Yeah, you too."

Once Liz left, Mattie strolled over to the music stand. Opening the CD case, she took out a CD and popped open the deck. There was time enough to think about the contest later. Right now, she was going to concentrate on the studio's upcoming dance concert. She had signed up for Liz's Modern Jazz class on her half days at school, which gave her a two hour break until she had to work at the desk.

At all the other in-studio concerts they'd had, she'd always performed to upbeat songs. They were her forte because they were the easiest to choreograph. Watching a three-hour coverage of an ice skating competition had given Mattie a new idea for the next concert. After pressing a button, she quickly moved to the middle of the room and posed in a temporary starting position. Seconds later, the haunting piano intro to Jewel's "Foolish Games" filtered through the speakers.

***

At approximately six-thirty, Tykota rode up on the motorcycle Zion Security had let him keep. Mattie had to smile because he looked so good on the high-tech silver speed machine. As she came outside, he pulled off his helmet and gave her a welcoming smile. Eyes as black as onyx darted quickly around the strip mall parking lot before resting once again on her. *One could leave the Navy SEALs, but the instincts would always remain,* she thought with an inward grin. Thick jet-black hair twisted into a braid and the bronzed features of his face stood out in sharp relief against the protective silver jumpsuit he wore, making him look like a dangerous astronaut. Swinging a leg over the seat, he stood up and enveloped her in a strong, gentle hug after she set the alarm and locked the door.

"Hello, my island beauty," he greeted in English, his voice low and deep.

"Hello, guardian of my heart," she responded.

Mattie felt more than heard the chuckle that rumbled deeply in his chest, and she hugged him tighter. God, how she loved this man.

"You brought the cycle," she observed, giving him one last squeeze.

"It was faster." He returned the squeeze, then caressed the back of her head.

Moving to the bike, he handed her a helmet and a protective jumpsuit. As she zipped up the jumpsuit and buckled her helmet, she watched as Tykota glanced around the parking lot again. He was a man of few words, always on the alert, always silently watching. Although she would never have the natural instincts he'd been born with, and the ones he'd honed during his SEALs stint, he'd taught her the fundamentals. And for that, she would always be grateful. Hoisting on her backpack, Mattie swung a leg over the seat. He put on his own helmet and started the ignition.

"What do you want to hear?" His voice came through the miniature speakers in the helmet.

"You choose this time," she offered, undecided.

He nodded. "Computer, scan for radio station The Zone, one-oh-one-point-five FM," he instructed.

"Scanning." There was a moment's pause and then, "Compliance. The Zone, one-oh-two-point-five FM." Seconds later, Hoobastank's latest ballad filtered through the headset. Sighing, Mattie loosened her grip on Tykota's waist and laid her head on his back as they raced towards home.

CHAPTER THREE

Decisions Made

Fountain Hills seemed like an isolated village nestled up against McDowell Mountain. Just a few miles outside of Fountain Hills, surrounded by waist-high rippling green grass, stood the home where Mattie and Tykota lived. The four bedroom, four bath stone and glass structure had been designed by Tykota and built by the company he used to work for, Zion Security. Of course, that was before he'd quit to start his own business, Black Hawk Protection Agency.

Zion employees, especially the active field agents, are given apartments within the Zion Headquarters compound. After Tykota had taken her from the island, they had lived there for almost two years. Despite the old adage of children being able to adapt to new surroundings, Mattie had not been able to cope. She had missed the open spaces of her island home, the smell of fresh air and pure ocean. So Tykota had found them a new place where there wasn't an ocean, but plenty of fresh air.

Mattie loved the home he had created for them. He'd designed a small dance studio for her, with one whole wall made of thick bulletproof glass, and another a wall of mirrors. Her own room wasn't really a room at all, but a screened off section of the house with a door that led to the backyard. She could hear the crickets chirping, the swishing sounds of the grass, stargaze, or watch lightning streak across the sky. One of the many things she missed most about the island of her birth was the violent storms. It didn't rain often in Phoenix, but when it did, Mattie had front row seats. Tykota came to a stop in the garage beside Mattie's Jeep. Pulling off the helmet and jumpsuit, she handed them to him, took a few steps from the cycle, and waited expectantly. When nothing happened a few minutes later, she frowned worriedly at Tykota.

"Where are the wolves?" she asked.

"Out playing, I imagine. I am sure they heard the cycle. Do not worry, sweetling. They know the boundaries," he assured her.

"I know, but they always greet us when we come home," she said, gazing out into the dark fields beyond their house.

"Not always, little one. Our land is big. There is much to explore. They know the boundaries," he repeated with a serene smile, heading towards the house.

Mattie followed at a slower pace, acknowledging that he was right. No matter how long they were out, Judah Earl and Dar Magnus always came back to the house because they knew there were humans to protect. Cole, one of Tykota's friends and fellow employee at the Agency, had brought them back from one of his assignments two years ago. The pair of wolves, brothers, had been released back into the wild for only two weeks when they had almost been killed again. There was still a small part of them that was wild, but not to the point where they would kill a human; unless it was a direct order, of course. Judah tended to stick close to Mattie whenever he could and Dar favored Tykota. However, they watched over both humans equally.

And they *did* know the boundaries. Mattie had watched Tykota set them up. Zion not only provided high tech security systems and personal protection, they also manufactured their own equipment. Tykota had planted four such security devices on their property. BDM's (Border Defense Mechanism) looked like sprinkler heads, and once activated, created an invisible and impenetrable barrier. Nothing, or no one, could get in or out without being detected. As for Judah and Dar, Tykota had slapped transmitter collars on them so every time they tried to exceed the barrier, the wolves would receive a gentle reminder that they were roaming too far.

Mattie felt like she was living in her own "house of the future". It had been a major icebreaker the first time she'd invited Ren and Mici over for a visit. She realized that her home life was not like the average teenager, and probably never would be thanks to Tykota's business, but she was happy. Once inside the house, Mattie headed back to her room.

"Lights on," she instructed, throwing her backpack on her desk.

She loved her room. It had taken her almost two months to get used to the fact that three of the four walls in her room were screens. Gray stone rose four feet off the ground, and instead of glass panes, window screens covered with bamboo-colored cloth curtains had been installed. A queen size bed covered with a comforter in the colors of sage green, butter yellow, lavender and sky blue dominated one side of the large room; a white velvet beaded canopy hung from the ceiling and draped lightly around the headboard. A chest of drawers made of smooth maple was stationed up against the wall at the foot of her bed, while a small make-up table and its cushioned bench took up space in the corner next to it.

Across the room, against one of the screened walls, a desk held a computer, photographs and some treasured childhood books. To the left of the desk, embedded in a wall of solid gray stone, was a full-length mirror. The mirror was unique in itself, for when Mattie touched a small panel next to it, the mirror moved to one side to reveal a walk-in closet. Even though there wasn't enough wall space to hang pictures or posters, it made her feel like she was sleeping outside. She remembered sleeping outside on a hammock back home, but that seemed like a lifetime ago.

"What do you want for dinner?" Tykota called from the family room.

"Why don't we order a pizza?" she called back. "Ren and Mici are coming over later and they'll probably end up spending the night."

"What kind of pizza?"

"Combo. We like everything," she yelled. "Except anchovies," she amended.

A second later, she glanced up to find him standing in the doorway. That was Tykota, quick and silent. Mattie couldn't remember how many times she'd thought he was in another room, only to turn around and discover his presence. She didn't know if it was part of his heritage, part of his training, or both. She just knew that it was what made him so unique.

"What time are they coming over?" he asked.

"I told Ren I would call her when I got home. Just order in about fifteen minutes and it should probably be here by the time they arrive," she said.

"It is a Friday night," Tykota pointed out.

Mattie paused in the act of toeing off her shoes. "Mmm, you're right. Better order it now."

"So does this mean that you are going to dance tomorrow?" he asked with a raised eyebrow.

Mattie released a little smile as she reached over and pulled her backpack onto the bed with her.

"Yeah, I guess it does. Liz brought it up and she gave me some background info on the situation. From what I gathered, you either become a regular or get a special pass," she explained.

Tykota waggled his head from side to side. "Sounds reasonable. I am going to order the pizza, then call for the boys. They have not come back yet," he said.

Mattie was instantly concerned. "You don't think something's happened to them, do you?"

Tykota didn't even justify that with an answer. With a look she'd seen many times before, he turned and walked away.

"Yeah, well, it's happened before," she mumbled under her breath, as though he had verbally responded to her question.

"Yes, but that was before I put in the BDM's." Tykota's voice floated back to her from down the hall.

She'd forgotten about the super audio sensory thing. He could probably hear two worms mating deep in the ground, his ears were that sensitive. As she emptied her backpack, Mattie turned her head to the flat thirty-two inch screen embedded in the stone wall at the end of her bed.

"Computer, display recording of today's episode of *Dance Jam Productions*," she instructed.

"Compliance," the voice intoned.

Seconds later, the screen flickered then cleared up in the middle of a newscast.

"…Horrifying discovery after attending a party the night before. Tonight, on *Channel Five News…*" Mattie propped herself against the headboard just as the introduction to the show started. The show's theme song, Kim Wilde's "Kids in America," began to play and the dancers leapt onto strategically placed risers to kick off Friday's segment of *Dance Jam Productions*.

***

"So…we came over for nothing?" Mici griped forty-five minutes later.

The three girls were sitting on the floor in Mattie's room, eating pizza.

31

"Why would you say something crazy like *that*?" Mattie retorted indignantly.

"Hel-lo? What's the use of going if we'll need partners?" Mici remarked.

"Oh, don't panic. They won't turn us away because we didn't come with guys. It just wouldn't be right," Mattie claimed.

"I can't believe Liz told you all that stuff. Y'all think it's true?" Ren wanted to know, eyes wide.

"Liz has never been known to lie about something like that. She's very serious about dance," Mattie said, biting into her slice of pizza.

"Did you watch today's episode?" Ren asked.

"Sure did," Mattie said around a mouthful of pizza

"So what time are we supposed to be there?"

"Sign up starts at eight, music starts at nine," she recited.

"Well, I hope you guys do great," Mici put in.

Mattie and Ren's pizza froze midway to their mouths. They stared at Mici in stunned silence, glanced at each other, then back at Mici. Ren released a teasing laugh.

"That's good, Mic. You almost had us there. 'Hope you guys do great'. That's cute. Real cute."

"It wasn't meant to be. I'm not entering the contest with you guys," Mici said with a straight face. "But I can do a quick reading if yo—"

"What the hell are you talking about?" Mattie interrupted. "You sure as hell are entering that contest with us."

Mici rolled her eyes. "Oh, c'mon, *cherie*. I've been trained in classical ballet. Sure, I like to dance, but this is different, more serious. A dance contest to be on our favorite show. What's up with that? It takes all the fun out of dancing altogether. Besides, do you know how many people are going to be at that thing tomorrow?" she pointed out.

Mattie scoffed and shook her head. "For heaven's sake, Mic, we're not trying out for a freakin' Broadway musical here. It's a dance show. A *dance* show. Where people go to have fun and dance. If anything, we'll get VIP passes out of the whole deal. Don't you want a VIP pass?" she cajoled in a hopeful tone. Mici shrugged. "We shall see tomorrow, *non*?"

***

The Ozone nightclub was jumping this Friday night. It was closing in on one a.m., after hours, and the music was already changing to techno. Through the smoky haze, a young man stood in a dark corner near the bar. Cigarette dangling from his fingers, he scoped out the people coming in the front door. Sighing, he took a lazy sip from the bottle of beer he was nursing.

He really didn't want to be here. It had been a long day at work and he'd been hoping to chill out on his couch at home. His coworkers assumed he was a partygoer, and most of the time he was, but not after a fifteen-hour workday. But he'd gotten another phone call. He took an angry draw on his cigarette and let it out between clenched teeth. He hated the phone calls and he hated what he had to do once he received one.

So here he was, at The Ozone, in a get up even his own mother wouldn't recognize him. He was good at disguises. He hadn't done the punk look in so long, he'd decided to try it out again: black leather pants, black biker boots and a black mesh, long-sleeved shirt. A spiked dog collar circled his neck and matching bands were clamped around his wrists. Freshly dyed platinum blonde hair had been gelled and was sticking out all over like he'd just rolled out of bed. Black eyeliner rimmed eyes with tinted brown contacts, and black fingernail polish adorned nails chewed to the quick.

Oh yes, he was good with disguises. So good, he was starting to forget what he really looked like.

"Time to go to work," he murmured.

Stabbing out his cigarette in a nearby ashtray, the young man detached himself from the corner. Pulling a stack of cards out of his back pocket, he began to circulate.

***

Saturday morning dawned sunny and warm. Eighty-three degrees, a slight cooling breeze, and a cloudless sky. For early March, in Phoenix, weather like that was a downright miracle. It was nowhere near cold, yet not hot enough to cook a four-course meal on the sidewalk. As Mattie stood outside in the huge mowed-out patch of backyard, she watched with a smile as Judah and Dar wrestled with one another.

Gracefully, she lowered herself to the grass, leaned back on her hands and raised her head to catch the breeze. She felt subtly energized after her Tai Chi lesson with Tykota. Their lesson was an early morning ritual that had started at the age of nine, when she had stumbled across him performing the exercise. She'd stuck to the lesson, in spite of the early morning hours, when she realized it kept her mind free of thoughts from...

Pale blue eyes moved to the sturdy oak tree located on the far edge of the property. Five white crosses surrounded the base of the tree, one for each family member that had been brutally taken from her. She would pay homage to them next week. She always did, at the same time, year after year. Time heals all wounds, or so she'd been told ad nauseam. Mattie passed a hand over her torso, eyes still focused on the oak tree.

Time might heal all wounds, she pondered, *but sometimes it left scars.* Shaking off the melancholy—there would be time for that soon enough—she hopped up and dusted off her bottom. She called for the wolves, which had wandered off during her moment of introspection. Judah and Dar came bursting through the tall grass as if they were racing to see who would reach her first.

"C'mon you guys. Let's go wake up the girls."

Sun Devil Stadium was located in the heart of downtown Tempe, snuggled right up against the Activity Center, with Arizona State University just on the other side. Mattie, Ren, and Mici arrived at seven forty-five, and the parking lot was already half full. Just looking at all the cars made Mattie wonder if all these people were coming to dance or just to watch. Finding a parking spot near the exit, the girls piled out and headed for the entrance. They climbed up a couple of steps to the bleachers to observe their surroundings.

At one end of the field was a stage, presumably where the hosts of *Dance Jam Productions*, Pepe Carrington and Sophie Brown, were going to MC the event; right behind the stage, sound technicians were setting up their equipment. Smack dab in the middle of the field, a large circle had been roped off with poles and yellow police tape.

"I guess that's where we're going to dance," Ren said.

"Looks like it," Mattie murmured, her eyes scanning the people around her.

"Where do you guys sign up?" Mici asked.

"I saw some signs pointing to the concession stands," Ren answered.

"Well, you guys had better hurry up," Mici advised. "It's almost eight o'clock and there's probably already a long line."

Mattie looked at her friend. "Are you sure you don't want to sign up with us?" she asked, relinquishing her purse.

Mici held her hands out to the sides and cocked her head to the side "Do I look like I'm dressed to dance?"

Wearing a beige, floral peasant blouse with flowing sleeves, blue hip-hugger jeans with a slight bell-bottom and platform mules, Mattie had to admit that that wasn't her usual dancing outfit. She had a different set of clothes for when they went out and this wasn't one of them.

"Okay. We'll look for you afterwards."

"Where are you going to be sitting?" Ren asked, dropping her own purse at Mici's feet.

Mici glanced around quickly before replying. "Right up in there a ways. High enough to see you guys," she said.

"Okay."

The three girls hugged, Mici wished them luck, and Mattie and Ren headed off to find the place to sign up. Just like Mici had predicted, there was a long line. They noticed a woman directing people into two lines, but couldn't understand what she was saying until they got closer.

"Couples over here, singles over there. If you're signing up as a couple, you need to be in this line. If you're here by yourself, you need to go over there," the woman droned on repeatedly.

Mattie and Ren moved into the Singles line and leaned against the wall. Mattie scrutinized the activity, dividing her attention between the people that were coming and the people that had just signed up. At times like this, she didn't feel self-conscious about her eyes; she was in a crowd, at an event where people had better things to do than stare at her. Although she gazed around, her eyes never lingered long on anyone or anything. After several quick probing searches, she could've described every person in the Couples line if asked.

Their own line moved slowly, and Mattie had to refrain from leaning out to see how long their line had become. Next to her, she felt Ren shift from foot to foot.

"Can you believe the injustice of being humiliated in public like this? A Singles line, for crissake. Who's lousy ass idea was *that*?" she griped. "I need a Marti. I should've brought a Marti. I can't *believe* I didn't bring any with me. That's not good. Marti's are my good luck charm. How can I get out there and dance if I haven't had a tiny, itty-bitty—"

Ren broke off abruptly as Mattie slashed her a look with her eyes.

"You need to take a deep breath and calm down before I have Mici conjure up a bottle of your apple juice and break it over your head," Mattie warned in a low tone.

Ren pursed her lips together, wondering for the quadrillionth time how her friend did it. *How could she be so calm, so...serene at a time like this, while she could feel the sweat breaking out under her armpits?* She hadn't gotten this hyped up since her last skateboard competition. And that had been six months ago.

Mattie returned her attention back to her surroundings, reflecting over Ren's nervous chatter. That's all it was too, just a release of nervous and excited energy. Mattie had never participated in a dance contest before, but this would be easy. Dancing was something she loved to do, and doing it in front of a lot of people came hand in hand with taking classes at Rhythm Station. It prepared you for events like this contest. If anything, she was ready for the whole ordeal to be over with so she could say that she'd tried.

Soon, she was as the counter, ready to sign up.

"Name?" the woman behind the counter requested.

"Mataya Black Hawk," Mattie said.

"Can you spell that, please?"

"M-a-t-a-y-a, last name is capital B-l-a-c-k capital H-a-w-k. It's two words," she enunciated.

"Address?"

"One-two-zero Palisades Highway."

"Phoenix?"

"No, Fountain Hills," Mattie corrected.

"Zip code?"

"Eight-five-two-six-eight."

"Phone number, area code first."

"Four-eight-zero-nine-nine-eight-two-seven-three-two."

The woman tapped some keys on her keyboard, then stepped away for a moment. When she came back, she slid a piece of paper across the counter with the number sixty-two painted in black.

"Okay, here's your number, miss. Peel it off and slap it on your back. You'll be partnered with someone before the music starts," the woman said.

Mattie was about to step away when she heard that last statement.

"Ex-excuse me. Did you say partnered?" she sputtered.

"Yes."

"Wha-uh…I didn't realize I was supposed to…come here…with someone," Mattie stuttered on. But of course, she *did* know. She'd watched the show and heard the requirements. Chris had mentioned it as well and there were couples here. Mattie supposed she'd have to chalk it up to her past. The idea of dancing with a guy she didn't know was a little unnerving, but she would just have to work through it.

"Well, you might not have to have a partner. It just depends on what the ratio is of single girls to single guys. We won't know until nine," the woman explained.

"Great," Mattie choked out hoarsely. *It's not like anything is going to happen in a crowd full of witnesses, anyway,* she thought. *And even if it did, things were different now.*

"Totally slammin'," Ren agreed.

"Hey everyone, thanks for coming out. We're the hosts of *Dance Jam Productions*, Pepe Carrington—"

"—And Sophie Brown. How are you guys doin' out there?"

The crowd at Sun Devil Stadium screamed, whistled, clapped and cheered. Excitement was running high. By the time nine a.m. had rolled around, almost one section of the bleachers had been filled with spectators. Mattie could no longer pick out Mici among them, but she did notice a couple of camera crews. She was pretty much pumped up like Ren now, and could feel the zing of excess energy waiting to be danced away.

Seeing Pepe and Sophie in person was a treat. Pepe was about five eight with brown hair cut short on the back and sides, but left long on top; despite the styling gel, a section of hair curled boyishly over his forehead. Thick eyebrows the same color as his hair shaded Mattie knew to be light green eyes, and a thin-lipped mouth constantly cracked sly smiles. He was in his early twenties, possessed an average build, not too thin, not too fat, and had a wicked sense of humor that always had Mattie laughing whenever she watched the show.

Sophie was a perfect foil for Pepe because she was just as crazy. She was a pretty, light-skinned African-American woman, also in her early twenties, who stood three inches shorter than Pepe. Her brown and blonde-streaked hair was worn Halle Berry-short, warm brown eyes sparkled with inner laughter, and her full mouth perpetually released ear-to-ear smiles. Her physique was the same as Mattie's, slim and toned, and she had a certain way of laughing that was infectious; a person just wanted to laugh because *she* was laughing.

She and Pepe got along so well, it was like watching her old favorite show *Moonlighting*. They fed off each other's energy, and, more often than not, would finish each other's sentences. There was speculation that they were an item, and Mattie secretly hoped that it was true. They looked good together and she could see them as a couple.

"Okay, so here's how it's gonna go down. We just got the results in from the sign up sheets and it looks like there's an even number of single girls and single guys," Pepe began.

Whistles and catcalls from the guys.

Whistles and shouts from the girls.

"So you single guys and single girls out there are going to have a dance partner," Sophie stepped in.

"Dandy," Mattie muttered under her breath.

"Righteous," Ren exclaimed with a wide smile.

"For every single girl that has a number, there is a guy that has that same number—" Pepe went on.

"—So all you have to do is find that person with your corresponding number and that person is your dance partner," Sophie finished.

"But first, let's explain the rules of the game," Pepe jumped in.

For the next fifteen minutes, Pepe and Sophie talked about the rules. A medley of Top Forty songs would be played and twelve finalists will be chosen. For Round Two, the twelve finalists will have to make up their own dance routines and perform them on the show next Friday. However, the music of choice had to be from a movie soundtrack. The group will then be narrowed down to six. Round Three is the Dance-Off, where each of the six finalists will be taught a dance routine by one of the *DJP* dancers. The routine will be performed on the show, where three couples will be chosen as regulars and the losers will get VIP passes.

Then the judges were introduced. Everyone went wild when they realized it was the *DJP* dancers. Ren nearly passed out from hysteria when she saw her beloved Chris Morrow.

"...So why don't we have the couples step outside the ring while the singles find their partners," Pepe was saying.

"Here we go," Mattie murmured under her breath.

"I hope my guy's gorgeous," Ren said, jumping up and down and clapping her hands. "Heck, I'd settle for just really, really cute," she added.

Mattie shook her head. *If the guys at the skate park could see her now,* she thought as she watched her friend hurry away. Although she couldn't help but think that Ren had a point.

"I would settle for someone with rhythm," she said around a laugh.

Moments later, her laughter faded completely when she turned around and came face to face with Jarek Thanos.

CHAPTER FOUR

Surprise, Surprise

M attie couldn't have been more shocked if her period had started while swimming in a public pool. As she squinted up at him, she desperately wished for the sunglasses she had left with Mici.

"Jarek?" she said in stunned disbelief.

Jarek would have recognized those piercing blue eyes anywhere. He whipped off his sunglasses and returned the same shocked expression.

"Mataya?" his surprised tone reflected hers.

Well, now that we got that *part out of the way*, she thought. "I can't believe this. You're number sixty-two?" she asked in disbelief.

"Yeah..." he trailed off, twisting his torso so she could get a look at his back.

"You're sixty-two, too?" he parroted.

"Yeah." Mattie found herself repeating the same action. She couldn't help herself. It was just too eerie.

"I didn't know you—"

"I didn't know you—"

They spoke simultaneously, stopped abruptly, and then laughed. Jarek chuckled again, tucking his sunglasses in the pocket of his cut-off sweats.

"You first," he said.

"I...was just going to say that I didn't know you danced. Or, *liked* to dance, that is..." Mattie trailed off and frowned, knowing that hadn't come out right.

Jarek smiled in understanding. He was pretty floored himself. "Yeah, I do. Love to dance, that is."

Mattie nodded once, nibbling on her bottom lip. "So…what were *you* going to say?"

"Aunt Liz didn't tell me you were coming out here today," he admitted.

"Well, I didn't really decide until last night," Mattie replied.

She forced herself not to fidget and decided to put her hands on her hips. Which, she soon realized, turned out to be her first mistake. The minute she did, she felt Jarek's eyes on her like a physical touch. His intense gaze suddenly made her feel naked. Her second mistake, of course, was the outfit itself. It hadn't seemed like a bad choice at the time. Tykota hadn't said anything and neither had her girlfriends. But then again, she wore outfits like this all the time to her dance class at Rhythm Station.

The red, black, and white top looked like a sleeveless wet suit right down to the zipper in front, but was made of spandex, not rubber. Her black lace-up spandex shorts would have been more appropriate for a music video entitled "Booty Call", and black and white wrestling shoes encased her feet. A red baseball cap with the initials ZSI emblazoned on it shielded her eyes and held back her braided ponytail.

The whole ensemble fit like a second skin and had been worn for the sole purpose of maximum mobility. What she wanted to hide was hidden and all the skin she wanted to show was exposed. Call her crazy, but Mattie would've bet her next paycheck that Jarek was wishing he had X-ray vision. She cursed mentally and wished again that her sunglasses weren't tucked beside Mici. If she'd had them she would've been able to study him freely, without detection, instead of making out-of-the-corner-of-her-eye glances.

Jarek was looking absolutely edible this fine Saturday morning. He probably could've been a spokesperson for Potato

Sacks "R" Us and started a whole new trend. He was dressed in deference to the weather in gray-cut off sweats over bike shorts, black jazz shoes (the ones that look like tennis shoes), white socks, and a white muscle shirt that had been raggedly cut into a half shirt. His attire yesterday had only given her a hint at what his body looked like. Today, however, was no longer a hint but the whole story.

His shorts showed off a pair of muscled thighs and calves, while his half shirt revealed a stomach that was six-packed and flatter than road kill. A white Old Navy baseball cap with his ponytail out the back completed a picture of a guy whose Drool Factor was off the scale. Mattie was doing a reasonable job of appearing unaffected, but she couldn't help but wonder why she'd never run into him before now.

"So, did you come here alone or with...someone?" Jarek broke the silence.

"I came with my girlfriends," Mattie responded, glancing at him quickly before turning to watch other people find their dance partners. "You?" she reciprocated.

"I came with my buddies, too. Did your friends sign up with you?" he asked.

"Just the one. Ren's around here somewhere, hoping to find her really, really cute dance partner," Mattie chuckled. "Her words, not mine."

Jarek laughed. "Yeah, my buddy, Gunner, is around here somewhere, too. His twin brother, Rader, likes to dance, but something like this would freak him out."

Mattie turned her eyes on him so suddenly that he froze. They were the first things he'd noticed about her when they'd met yesterday.

"What?" he asked warily. "What did I say?"

"N-nothing. I...just thought I was experiencing déjà vu or something," she murmured.

"Why do you say that?" he inquired, hoping he hadn't upset her in some way.

"One of my friends didn't audition for almost the same reason. Except her excuse had been 'I'm a classically trained ballet dancer and auditioning for my favorite show would take all the fun out of dancing'", Mattie explained with a small smile.

"Wouldn't it be weird if my friend, Gunner, ended up being your friend's dance partner and his twin ended up sitting next to your friend?" Jarek said with a crooked smile.

Yeah right. Mici would've gotten a kick out of that, she mentally scoffed. *She'd probably chalk it up to the planets being in retrograde or something. Weird? I don't think so. Try freaky-deaky.*

"It would be downright scary," she said aloud, trying to keep a shudder of apprehension at bay.

There was no way she was going to admit that she'd been thinking the same thing. This whole situation was just plain eerie. If Mattie didn't know any better, she would have thought that Liz had arranged for them to meet. It was strange to think that she already had something in common with this person even though they hadn't really said anything significant. Mattie opened her mouth to ask another question, but Pepe began to talk.

"Okay, so we all got partners now?" he shouted into the microphone. "Cool, cuz I got my partner right here." He put his arm around Sophie and gave her an enthusiastic hug.

"Are you guys ready to dance?" she yelled into her microphone, a wide smile creasing her face.

Shouts and clapping rippled though the people in the circle.

"Cool. So why don't we find out what our deejay's got planned for you guys," Pepe said.

They walked over to a guy that was standing behind a turntable, bopping his head to the music on his headphones.

"This is Deejay Flipside. You might not recognize the face, but you'll recognize his music..." Pepe began.

"...Because we borrowed him from The Storm Room," Sophie stepped in.

The crowd became rowdy again at the mention of a popular teen nightclub. Mattie laughed and clapped her hands. *How did they do that? She* wondered. *They acted like sports commentators, switching back and forth so quickly it made it seem like only one person was talking instead of two.*

"What've you got for our contestants, Mr. Deejay?" Pepe asked in a dramatic game show host voice.

"Do you think they have to practice that?" Mattie asked aloud.

Jarek was laughing, too, and shaking his head.

"I doubt it. It seems too easy to be practiced," he said.

"W'sup, w'sup, w'sup y'all," Deejay Flipside said into the mike.

The crowd responded with hoots and yells.

"Deejay Flipside is gonna start y'all off at high speed with La Bouche and Sixty-Nine Boyz. Tupac and Dr. Dre are gonna perform a chillectomy on y'all and then we're gonna get a little sexy with Madonna. That all right witch y'all?" he said.

Mattie and Jarek glanced at one another. "Not a bad mix of music," she murmured.

"Yeah," he agreed.

"I wonder what song he's going to play by Madonna?" Mattie pondered. "She has a lot of...good songs."

Jarek shrugged a shoulder. "Who knows?"

"Okay, so y'all ready to bust a move?"

A chorus of "Oh yeah's" rippled across the people in the circle.

"You ready, partner?" Jarek asked with a blinding smile.

His smile, as well as the excitement emanating from him, was contagious. Mattie returned it tenfold.

"Yep, yep," she drawled.

"Good luck to all you dancers out there," the deejay said, before slipping on his headphones. "The rules are—"

"There *are* no rules," Pepe and Sophie jumped in.

"Do whatever makes you feel good, just make sure it's clean. The judges will let you know if what you're doing is too dirty," Sophie continued. "We're PG-13 here, ladies and gents, not Skinemax."

"Yeah, so no naked bodies," Pepe added with a sly wink and a waggle of eyebrows.

"So let's kick it!" they yelled simultaneously.

The music came on and Mattie and Jarek began to dance. *So far, so good*, she thought, watching his body move. The beat was quick but Mattie wanted to pace herself. Her favorite dance song was "Tootsie Roll" by the Sixty-Nine Boyz, and she usually went all out whenever she heard that song. Mattie noticed that Jarek was pacing himself as well. *At least he has rhythm,* she thought with relief.

By the time Mattie heard the beginnings of her favorite song, she was warmed up and ready to go. The song came on and Mattie let herself go. And she was happy to see that Jarek could keep up. Suddenly, he stopped dancing, crossed his arms over his chest, shifted his weight to one leg and watched her with a sexy half-smile on his lips. She glanced over at him and almost stopped dancing herself when she saw him staring at her. Then she noticed the smile and burst out laughing.

"You'd better quit," she chided, lightly punching him on the shoulder.

"I dunno if I can keep up with you, girl," Jarek teased, shaking his head.

In a bold move she knew she never would've done under normal circumstances, Mattie sidled up to him until she could feel his breath on her face. Putting her arms around his neck, she swiveled her hips from side to side as she moved up and down his body.

"You're not saying you're tired already, are you? So much for stamina," she scoffed and rolled her eyes.

Jarek tilted his head to one side, pushing his tongue into his cheek as though he was trying not to laugh. It was a teasing yet subtle remark against his manhood, and he wasn't about to let her get away with it. Staring directly into her pale blue eyes, he began to match the movement of his hips with hers. His Aunt Liz had said that Mattie was an excellent and natural dancer. He had to agree, for on a scale of one to ten, she was a twenty.

He slowly uncrossed his arms and slipped them around her waist, all the while keeping eye contact with her. Pulling her closer, he released a slow smile.

"I'll show you stamina, Blue Eyes," he said in a low, silky tone.

Mattie opened her mouth to reply, but her throat closed up when Jarek positioned his right leg between both of hers. His embrace became firmer as they danced low to the ground, then back up. Standing upright once again, Jarek swung her into a low dip right in sync to Madonna's "Human Nature."

Mattie released a joyous laugh as the song played on. It was meant to be a cool-down number she knew, but it was doing just the opposite. She glanced around at the other dancers to find the majority of them dancing the way she had with Jarek. She was surprised at that, for she was always aware of her immediate surroundings. But her gaze hadn't strayed once since she'd started dancing with Jarek.

Her attention had been focused solely on him the entire time, which again, was unusual for her. She found it difficult to relax with anyone of the opposite sex for long periods of time. Except for Tykota and his men, of course. She and Jarek danced close together for the rest of the song and Mattie never once felt panic rise. The way he held her was non-threatening; firm enough that she wouldn't fall if they tried a new step, yet loose enough that she could move away.

Jarek really was a great dancer. He never did the same step twice, she noticed. Mattie especially liked the way he swiveled his hips, which he did a lot. Not a Ricky-Martin-shake-your-bon-bon kind of swivel, but more of a smoldering Enrique-Iglesias- I've-got-you-in-my-trap sort of swivel. He had a sexy hip roll that fairly shouted "Male Stripper" through seventeen foot Woofers. The song ended and everyone clapped. Jarek and Mattie both were slightly out of breath.

"So, how many pounds do you think you guys lost?" Sophie yelled into her mike.

Mattie laughed because she had been thinking the same thing. "At least twenty," she retorted jokingly.

Jarek laughed. "No kiddin'".

"You guys looked smokin' out there," Pepe jumped in. "Ready for a break?"

That was met with some heartfelt responses.

"Cool. We're gonna take a fifteen minute break while we tally up the scores here. Drinks and snacks are being served at the refreshment stands if you guys didn't bring water bottles," Pepe announced.

"Did you bring something?" Jarek asked, removing his hat.

Mattie watched as he took down his ponytail, ran his fingers through his hair, wiped the sweat off his forehead with the back of his forearm, then put the hat on backwards. She blinked, realized that she was blatantly staring, and looked away. *What had he asked?* She wondered. *Oh, right, the water bottle.*

"Uh, yeah, I did. But it's up in the stands with Mici," she answered.

Jarek narrowed his eyes as he sat down. Or maybe it was her overactive imagination.

"My Mama taught me how to share," he said, holding up an insulated canister that Mattie had to failed to see when he'd first come up to her.

"Yeah. Thanks. It was stupid of me to leave it. Too excited, I guess," she said, crossing her legs and falling gracefully on the ground.

Jarek unscrewed the cap and gave it to her first. She took a couple of swallows before handing it back to him. She watched him swallow, screw the cap back on and set it aside.

"So, who's Mici?" he asked with studied casualness.

Definitely not her overactive imagination, she thought. He was wary all of a sudden and Mattie couldn't fathom why. She was pretty sure she'd mentioned coming with her girlfriends.

"The girlfriend I told you about," she reminded him. "You know, the classically trained ballet dancer?"

In the blink of an eye, his face relaxed into an easy smile and he reached over to tug on her braid. Mattie tilted her head back. Now it was her turn to be wary. *Why the attitude change?* She wondered. *Surely he wasn't...*Mattie blocked the outrageous thought from her mind. *You're really reaching here, Mataya,* she chided mentally. *Your hat must've sealed in the heat for too long.*

"...Really well," Jarek was saying.

Mattie shook her head, then tugged on the bill of her cap. "Sorry, Jay, I missed that," she admitted, feeling the red heat of embarrassment stealing up her cheeks.

Jarek cocked his head slightly and stared at her with a half smile on his lips.

Mattie shifted nervously, trying to remember what she'd said to garner such blatant scrutiny.

"What?" she demanded when the silence continued.

Jarek's smile grew as he shook his head. "Nothing, really. It's just that no one's ever called me Jay before. Not even my friends. I usually just go by J.T."

"Does...does that bother you? I didn't know-"

"No, no. It's all right. Really. I don't mind at all," he interjected softly, his gaze becoming more intent.

Mattie nodded once. "Okay. Coolness. And I usually just go by Mattie. So...what did you say before?"

"I said that you dance really well," he repeated.

"Thanks. I have a great teacher."

"My aunt?" he guessed.

"Yep. You?"

Jarek waved his hand in the air. "Nah. Fifty percent natural and fifty percent observation. After a few hours of practice, I can pretty much catch onto anything," he said.

"I take a Modern Jazz class that your aunt teaches. But music itself has been a constant in my life for as long as I can remember. It consisted of steel drums, bongos, chants, and other handmade instruments no one has ever heard of. I wasn't exposed to dance music until I was about..." Mattie paused to think. "...Probably eleven, definitely twelve. I started watching MTV a lot. Ren and Mici, my best friends, got me hooked on *Dance Jam*. And then I got the job at Rhythm Station," she concluded.

Jarek nodded. "Interesting. Where are you from?"

"Maui," she stated.

And then she immediately closed down. Jarek could see the change happening in her face. She tugged on the end of her braid and looked away, a classic end of story gesture. Definitely interesting. Mataya intrigued him like no other female. He knew from talking to his Aunt Liz that she was a very private person who hardly talked about herself. Liz still didn't know that much about her despite the fact that she'd been working with the girl for nearly a year. She definitely had a story to tell and Jarek had always liked a challenge.

"Would you like to go out sometime? Dancing, I mean," he offered.

Mattie turned her gaze back to him, studying him silently, and he absently wondered from which parent she got her pale blue eyes. They were stunning, really, the first thing anyone would notice when looking at her. She had a way of gazing at you like she was peering into your soul. He'd never known anyone to have eyes that color, but he liked them. And he liked *her*.

"Sure. That sounds like fun," she answered.

Jarek beamed back at her and opened his mouth to respond, but Pepe's voice reached out to them through the speakers.

"You guys pretty much cooled down now?" he said into the mike.

The response was less enthusiastic than it had been earlier, but, despite being tired, everyone was still psyched.

"Great. Well, I believe we're ready now, so pull up some green carpet and take a chill pill. First of all, we'd like to thank you all for signing up today," he stopped to clap.

"And we'd like to thank you all out in the stands for comin' out and supporting these people," Sophie added, also clapping her hands.

The cheering in the stands was almost deafening.

"Yes, yes, yes. We didn't realize *DJP* had such a loyal following until today. We'd also like to thank Deejay Flipside for spinnin' the tunes," Pepe said, giving the deejay a cocky two-fingered salute.

"Okay everyone, here we go," Pepe and Sophie shouted at the same time.

Mattie put her hands in her lap to hide her crossed fingers. It was a long shot, she knew. There'd been such a big turnout it would be crazy to think she and Jarek would have a chance.

"When you hear your number, walk with a quickness up here to the stage so everyone can get a look at ya," Sophie joked with an exaggerated wink.

"Couple number twenty-four, c'mon down," Pepe announced in his best Bob Barker voice.

Mattie screamed wildly and pumped her fist in the air when she saw Ren and her dance partner make their way up to the stage. And then she almost passed out from shock when she heard Sophie enthusiastically announce, "Finalist number nine…couple number sixty-two, c'mon down."

CHAPTER FIVE

Sunday

"Okay, so Mattie gave me the idea the other day of watching pairs skating to get ideas for lifts. And she was so kind to supply the tapes," Liz was saying.

Mattie and Jarek had decided to meet Liz at the studio. Sundays were the only days that Rhythm Station was closed, which gave the two teenagers a chance to start on their dance routine. Mattie was still experiencing delayed shock about being a finalist. She and Ren had acted crazy on stage the other day, hopping up and down, screaming, with their arms wrapped around one another. She'd practically had to hold her friend up when Chris Morrow had come up to congratulate them. And her body was still tingling from Jarek's exuberant off-the-ground bear hug. The gesture had been instinctive she knew, a handshake hadn't seemed appropriate, but she hadn't felt threatened. Not for an instant. All in all, Mattie was glad she had ended up with Jarek as a partner. She didn't think she would've felt comfortable with anyone else.

Too bad she still was a bit uncertain about doing the lifts. Not that she was afraid of heights, but the idea of being lifted over the head of someone she'd just met, wasn't exactly the best getting-to-know-you gesture.

"So why do we have to do lifts in this routine, anyway?" she complained grudgingly.

Slouched in the corner of the lobby couch, she tucked her legs beneath her and gave Liz a pouty glare. It was all in good fun, and Liz knew she was kidding, but there was still that small feeling…

Liz gave an exaggerated huff, shifted her weight to one hip, and leaned her arm across the top of the television set she'd wheeled in.

"Because Jarek wants to feel manly," she retorted with a straight face.

"*What?*" he cried indignantly. "That's a bunch of bullsh—"

"Just kidding," Liz trilled.

Mattie burst out laughing, watching as he settled back with one last mutinous glare at Liz.

"Seriously, though, Mattie. He has to show them he's strong enough to do them. He might be your partner, but it's possible he'll have to lift someone else. You've seen the dancers perform the group routines," she pointed out.Mattie

sighed and leaned her head back. "Yeah, I guess," she sighed again.

"Mataya, how badly do you want to be a regular?" Jarek asked quietly.

Mattie rolled her head to look at him, momentarily sidetracked at the way her name tripped off his tongue. Hardly anyone called her by her full name. She was pretty sure she'd told him to call her Mattie, but she found she liked the way he said it better.

"Not as badly as the other eleven finalists," she admitted. *And not if it meant he discovered her secret.*

"Then we won't do the lifts," he shot back in a decisive tone.

"*What?* Wait a minute, Mattie—" Liz began to protest.

"But how badly do *you* want to be a regular, Jay? I mean, is this something you've dreamt about? Something you've worked towards? "Cuz I'll tell you right now, that audition was no big deal for me. I don't think I even really wanted to do it. It's just dancing for me. It's another way to do something that I love to do anyway. I'd be happy with a VIP Pass," she paused to study his face. Then she shrugged. "But that's how *I* feel."

Jarek, who was slouched at the other end of the sofa, ran a hand over his head. He was dressed in olive-colored warm-up pants and a white tank top today. His hair was pulled back in a ponytail, and he absently tugged the end of it when he ran his hand over his head again. On the one hand, he'd done it for fun, too. He loved to dance, so why not try a dance contest? On the other hand, being chosen as a finalist, out of all those other people, had been luck. Pure dumb luck. This opportunity would be good exposure for the both of them. It could lead to something better, more lucrative, in the future. And it wouldn't look too bad on his resume, either. But if they didn't make it to the Dance-Off round, he wanted to show those judges why they should've been.

"I more or less feel the same way you do," he replied after a long moment.

"You guys," Liz groaned, burying her head in her arms.

"But I am *not* about to get out there on Friday with a half-as—"

Liz's head jerked up. "Jarek Logan Thanos," she barked a warning.

"—Baked dance routine," he quickly amended with an apologetic glance in Mattie's direction.

Mattie giggled in amusement.

"You weigh—what? One-oh-five max?" he continued.

Mattie shrugged. "Yeah. Something like that, I guess."

She'd never been obsessive about her weight. The only time she got on a scale was at the doctor's office. And since she rarely got sick, she had no idea what she weighed. She was petite, true, but she had some muscle tone, too.

"No problem," Jarek was saying. "I bench more than that at the gym. We can do a dance routine without lifts, but it won't look as good. Especially if the other finalists are planning on doing them. That's how *I* feel," he concluded.

Liz turned her gaze to Mattie, one eyebrow raised.

"I guess the question is whether you trust J.T. He's going to be lifting you over his head and dipping you about an inch from the floor. Do you trust him enough not to drop you?" she asked.

Mattie's eyes became hooded as she stared at Liz for a long moment, then switched to Jarek. She searched his face openly, probed deeply into his eyes, and was pleased when he didn't flinch or look away. She wasn't used to this. She wasn't used to being in close contact with the opposite sex. At least, not with someone her own age. She was used to baby boys, toddlers, and hugs from Tykota and his best friends. But Jarek was different. He was a boy who was interested in her as a friend. Possibly as more than a friend, she suspected. And she really wasn't ready to open that part of herself up yet. Was she?

It's not like he can hurt you, she rationalized mentally. *At least, not physically. He could try of course, but then he'd be flat on his back before he could blink. You're comfortable with him, Mattie. Just keep yourself covered up and you'll be fine.*

Jarek watched as clear eyes scanned his body, lingering on his chest and arms, before flicking over his legs. Her expression was unreadable, something he knew she didn't have to work too hard to do. He didn't realize he'd been holding his breath until she finally spoke.

"I don't really know you, the *real* you, but I expect I will this coming week. I'm comfortable with you, but, well, let's jut see where the day takes us," she said softly.

Well, you can't ask for more than that, he thought with a nod. *It's better than an outright no.*

He glanced at Liz. "Let's get started, then. We still have to choose the tunes."

For the next three hours, Jarek and Mattie watched the programs from some of the best pair's skaters and ice dancers in the world. The long and short programs from Elena Bechke and Denis Petrov, Ekatarina Gordeeva and Sergei Grinkov, Isabelle Brasseur and Lloyd Eisler, Jamie Sale and David Pelletier, and Kyoko Ina and John Zimmerman gave them ideas for lifts. The free dance performances from Rene Roca and Gorsha Sur, Schae-Lyn Bourne and Victor Kraatz, Jarrod Swallow and Elizabeth Punsalan, Marina Anassina and Gwendel Pezeraut, and Jane Torvill and Christopher Dean introduced them to style and grace.

Jarek particularly like Kraatz and Bourne's method of skating because of their hydroblading technique; a move that had them both gliding mere inches from the ice. But that wasn't the only reason he was enjoying it. He was being allowed a glimpse into Mattie's life. She loved ice-skating. She sat immobilized, barely moving as if she were afraid she might miss something. Seeing as how these were her videotapes, Jarek got the impression she knew every arm movement and every triple jump by heart. Yet the more he watched, the more he realized why she loved the sport so much.

The skaters made it look so effortless, it was hard to believe they would practice for several hours, even days, on just one element. The spins, the jumps, the footwork, the costumes, and the music blended together to make a point. It was all about teamwork and trust. Jarek could see that now. The female had to have complete trust in her partner; trust him enough not to drop her once he got her over his head or down near the ice. Of course, they would be nowhere near any ice, but the concept was still the same.

During their lunch break, Liz, Mattie and Jarek discussed certain aspects of the routines they had watched. And then another door in Mattie's life opened for him. Not only did she love ice-skating, she knew all the technical terms that went along with the sport. He didn't know the difference between a triple axel and a triple salchow, let alone how they were able to jump high enough do them. But Mattie knew and could even tell if the skater was going to mess up.

"...Lifts, J.T.?" Liz was saying.

Jarek blinked and looked down at his sandwich.

"Sorry, Liz. What did you say?" he asked sheepishly.

Mattie chuckled as Liz sighed and rolled her eyes.

"I said, did you get any ideas for lifts?" Liz repeated.

"Yeah, actually, I did. I realize we can't do all of them. Probably not even half of'em, but some of them had a pretty basic entry and exit method," he commented, smiling inwardly at the skating terminology he'd just used. He'd been paying attention to the commentary more than he'd thought.

"Okay. So which ones do you think you might be able to do without dropping me?" Mattie inquired.

Jarek threw his napkin at her in response to the teasing comment, but he noticed that the amusement didn't quite reach her eyes. She was serious.

"That one Russian pair where the girl looked like a doll?"

"Gordeeva and Grinkov?" Mattie confirmed.

"Yeah. They had that one where he lifted her up and behind his head while her legs were spread out—"

"—And then she moved one leg over his shoulder and he sorta pushes it out of the way—" Mattie jumped in again.

"—Making it into a one-handed lift," Jarek concluded, nodding his head.

Mattie was nodding enthusiastically even before he'd finished the sentence.

"Yeah, that's a basic overhead lift that all the pairs skaters do. That over-the-shoulder thing was just a different way of performing the lift," she said. "Creativity breeds higher score."

She flashed a quick glance at him before biting into her sandwich. "Do you think you'll, sorry, *we'll* be able to do that one?"

"Yeah, I do," he shot back without hesitation.

"Good," Mattie garbled around a mouthful of food. "What else?"

"Marval and Urbanski sure are a daring duo," he commented casually.

Liz's straw froze halfway to her mouth and her eyes went wide.

Mattie's chewing paused for half a second and *her* eyes were burning a hole in his forehead.

Jarek cleared his throat, ran a hand through his hair and frowned. *Was it something I said?*

"There is no way on God's green earth that you're going to *attempt*—"

"I would have to know you since *childhood* before I would let you—"

"Okay, stop," Jarek raised his voice over the protests, slicing his hand in the air.

Liz and Mattie had spoken simultaneously and at a decibel that would've rousted the occupants of a cemetery in the next county. The silence, however, was instantaneous. Jarek quickly took advantage of it before either one of them could get their second wind.

"It was an observation, okay? A simple...spectator-like observation. The things they did were too dangerous and would be *way* over the top for a dance routine," he began to explain. "Hey, I may be cocky sometimes, but I'm not crazy. It would take years and years of practice, and years and years of partnership to try some of that stuff. However, I *did* like that move where her stomach rested on his hand, while the other was holding her arm out." He demonstrated with his own hands.

Mattie nodded in understanding. "Yeah. That's called The Helicopter," she answered.

"Which kinda looks like that other basic overhead lift. Where she's facing her partner and he lifts her over his head. One leg is usually bent at the knee, arms are widespread," Liz added.

Jarek pointed his finger in the air. "Yeah. And the one where she leapt into his arms."

"Leap of Faith," Mattie supplied.

"But that move looks so much better on a seamless motion, y'know? I mean, he can keep her in that lowered position for a few seconds because they're still moving," Liz retorted in her dance instructor's voice.

"So we'll slap on some rollerblades," Jarek teased with a light punch to Mattie's arm.

Mattie giggled around her straw and shook her head.

"Yeah, ha-ha, J.T. Very funny. I think something like *that* would be a little over the top. Even for this," Liz said wryly.

"Look, I know what my limitations are, guys. I mean, the majority of the stuff they did wouldn't look near as good on the floor as it does on the ice. But then again, there's a lot of stuff we could copy, change around, or choreograph ourselves. And Mattie is so petite, I won't have any problems lifting her. If anything, I'll have to tone down my strength to accommodate her weight," Jarek expounded, encompassing both females in his gaze.

"Okay, Mr. Universe," Mattie joked. "We wouldn't want you to break a tank top strap or anything."

"Why you little..." Jarek laughed and reached across the table as though he was going to grab her.

Mattie laughed along with him, deflecting his attempt at contact with a move that was as much a part of her as breathing. The force of pressure had been tempered to that of a light slap, but the outcome would've been unpleasant if Jarek's intentions had been anything but playful.

Jarek and Liz hid their stunned expressions. Barely. Liz had expected her to dodge away from him. *He'd* expected some kind of female oh-stop-that type of shriek. Instead, he'd encountered Grasshopper's kid sister. He'd seen that same move many times. In a Steven Seagal flick.

"Where'd you learn how to do that?" he blurted without thinking.

Mattie's eyebrows went up. "Do what?"

"That karate block move you just did."

"Tykota."

"Tykota," he repeated flatly.

Mattie nodded, a smile forming on her lips. Jarek opened his mouth to ask who exactly *was* this Tykota person, but Liz began to pick up her hamburger wrappings.

"Okay guys. Time to get back to work," she instructed briskly. "I was thinking that we could set up the video cam and get some lifts on tape for you all to incorporate later."

Mattie stood and began to pick up her own garbage. "That sounds cool. Besides, I have plans later on."

With Tykota no doubt, Jarek mentally scoffed. He didn't know why he felt jealous. He didn't know why he should have this sudden incredible urge to beat this faceless guy to a pulp. Of course, he could be overreacting. This guy could be her instructor, or her older brother, or just another one of her best friends. Back at the studio, with the camera's eye trained on them, Jarek focused his attention on their routine.

It was almost five o'clock by the time they finished and Mattie felt she and Jarek had accomplished quite a lot. She had no qualms about doing the lifts with him now. His grip had been firm yet gentle and he had adapted easily to the different lifts they'd tried. Although she had teased Jarek about toning down his strength, she soon realized he'd spoken the truth. The first couple of attempts, he'd thrown her up in the air like a child. After that, the lifts had become easier, the ideas faster and faster. A dance routine was beginning to take shape. She was a little tired, a little sore, but she was satisfied with their progress.

Mattie closed down the studio since Liz had left hours ago, while Jarek waited outside.

"We got a lot done today," he said, walking her to her Jeep.

"Sure did. Now all we need to do is make up some steps and choose the music," she said, searching in her purse for her keys.

Jarek checked out Mattie's Jeep Cherokee as he strode by her side. It was a sparkling white hard top with limo dark windows and license plate that read WOLFGRL.

"So, you're into wolves, huh?" he asked, leaning against the driver side of his own car.

Mattie unlocked the passenger door and stowed her duffel bag on the floor of the front seat. Slipping on her sunglasses, she glanced over her shoulder at him.

"What?" she asked, closing the door.

Jarek felt a momentary pang of disappointment that she'd shielded her eyes, but he pushed it away. "Your license plate. You're into wolves? I've heard they can be dangerous," he commented.

"You've been watching too much Wild Kingdom," Mattie joked.

"More like National Geographic," Jarek cracked.

Mattie tilted her head to one side. "They're only dangerous when they're hungry or provoked by humans. More often than not, hunters are always trying to kill them and their babies. But they're very beautiful creatures and have wonderful protective instincts."

"That sounds like the voice of experience."

Mattie smiled that smile Jarek had started thinking of as her I-know-something-you-don't-know smile.

"It is. I have a couple at home," she replied.

Jarek blinked in surprise and straightened away from the door. "You...you have a couple of...wolves? As pets?" he stuttered in disbelief.

Mattie nodded, her smile growing wider. She made her way to the driver's side and hopped in. She rolled the passenger window down halfway so she could see him.

"Liz is getting a temp to take my place this week so we can work on our routine. Can you meet me here after school tomorrow to discuss music?" she asked.

"Yeah. Um, that sounds cool," Jarek answered vaguely, his mind still on the wolf issue.

He nodded, hiding his perplexed expression behind the sunglasses he just slipped on. He really was gorgeous, Mattie thought. Gorgeous *and* non-threatening. Now there was a combination worth keeping.

"See you tomorrow then," she said aloud, then rolled up the window and pulled away.

CHAPTER SIX

Monday

"So, who was that perfect specimen of male humanity you were dancing with Saturday morning?"

"Where *were* you all day Sunday?"

"And Sunday night?"

It was Monday afternoon, second period lunch. The three girls were sitting in the hallway of the Drama building, bombarding Mattie with questions. Mattie held up a hand and gave them both a warning look of silence.

"One question at a time. Please," she said slowly.

"The perfect specimen of humanity," Ren jumped in quickly. "Who was he?"

"Jarek Thanos. Liz's nephew," Mattie answered.

Ren squeezed her hands together and bounced knees that were crossed Indian-style. "Liz's nephew, huh? Can he jam?" she asked excitedly.

"He can jam," Mattie replied with a sly smile. *Boy,* could he jam.

"A guy like that had *better* have some rhythm," Ren said, jabbing the air with an index finger.

"Yeah, and if you're as talented as Liz, rhythm is a genetic requirement," Mici added, popping a grape into her mouth.

"So what are you guys—" Mattie broke off abruptly, tilted her head, and frowned at Ren. "Who's *your* guy?"

"Jamie Zane. Freshman at ASU," she said with a pursed smile and a waggle of eyebrows.

Mici's jaw dropped down. Mattie had a hard time keeping her own mouth from swinging open, but she managed. Barely.

"A college man, *mon ami? Mon Dieu,* I couldn't have done any better myself," Mici said after the initial shock had worn off.

"Yeah, but how does he feel about a three-sixty, fakie ally-oop grind on a half pipe?" Mattie tossed out.

Mici threw her head back and roared with laughter, while Ren recovered from almost choking on a spoonful of yogurt. Taking a sip from her ever-present bottle of sparkling apple juice, Ren threw a searing glare at her friend.

"First of all, *that* little trick doesn't even exist," she retorted drolly with a shake of her head.

Good Lord, she thought. *What with all the lingo I toss around and all the Xtreme Games on ESPN I've forced them to watch, you'd think they'd remember some of the tricks.*

"Second, I never mentioned it. I said I was into skating. He assumed I meant *ice* skating," Ren paused to shrug. "I didn't bother to correct him Besides, I didn't really like him at first. And then the music started."

Ren didn't have to finish the thought. The look on her face and the smile that creased her mouth said it all. Jamie Zane had been a pleasant surprise and Mattie knew exactly how she felt. For the first time, in a long time, she hadn't cringed or felt threatened. She hadn't wanted to run and hide. Of course, times had changed. She was no longer a helpless and defenseless seven-year-old child.

"Hey Mic, you weren't sitting next to a guy named Rader, were you?" Mattie asked, suddenly.

"No. Why? Was he cute?" she countered, stretching her legs out and throwing her skirt over her knees.

Mattie shrugged. "I dunno. But with a name like that, one can only hope. Especially if he's a friend of Jarek's."

"A friend of Jarek's was in the stands? And I *missed* him?" Mici claimed indignantly.

"So he says. His friend's twin brother—"

"*Twin brother?*" Mici and Ren cried simultaneously.

"I missed twin brothers in the stands," Mici murmured forlornly.

"No, you only missed Rader in the stands. His twin, Gunner, was out there dancing," Mattie said with a chuckle.

"That name sounds familiar," Mici murmured thoughtfully.

"He's one of the twelve finalists," Mattie supplied.

"Personally, I don't remember a friggin' thing after we got chosen. That whole day is nothing but a blur to me," Ren said with a shake of her head.

"Including the moment you got all moony-eyed over meeting Chris Morrow?" Mattie wanted to know.

Ren let out a short bark of laughter. "Well, maybe not *all* of it was a blur," she conceded.

"Ditto," Mattie agreed. She knew she'd never forget that hug.

"So, where were you yesterday?" Mici wanted to know.

"At the studio with Jarek and Liz, getting ideas. I brought in some ice skating tapes and we watched them."

"So, what, you guys gonna perform on rollerblades?" Ren joked.

"Yeah, ha-ha, goofus. Lifts Ren. Ice skaters, pairs in particular, do some pretty cool lifts. I thought that would be a good place to start for ideas," Mattie explained.

Ren nodded. "Wish I'd thought of that first. I have no idea what Jamie and I are gonna do. I'll have to call him and see. Have you guys chosen a soundtrack yet?"

"Actually, I'm meeting him today after school at the studio to do just that," Mattie answered.

"Do you think it'll be hard? I mean, your tastes are so eclectic, Mattie, it's eerie," Mici said.

Mattie nudged her with her foot and let out a sound that was half-snort, half-giggle. "Eclectic? Is that your word of the day, Mic?" she teased.

Mici turned her face in profile and raised her chin at a haughty angle. "I am trying to expand my vocabulary, *mon ami*. With Mrs. Hedley's new cache of words, I will be able to stretch the boundaries of my learning tentacles," she recited.

A short moment of silence, then the three girls burst out laughing.

"Learning tentacles? I thought I'd never hear you compare yourself to an octopus, Mici," Ren drawled around a chuckle.

"'Cache of words'. I like that," Mattie added, leaning against the wall with an amused sigh.

"It's French, you know," Mici pointed out.

"We know," Mattie and Ren said simultaneously, then laughed again.

Mattie sighed once more, in content this time, and pulled out a package of cookies; Fudge mint cookies, to be exact. Keebler's Fudge Shoppe Grasshopper cookies were her I-need-help-making-a-decision-give-up-for-Lent-Aunt-Flow's-monthly-visit-you're-grounded-I'm-taking-away-your-privileges-you'd-better-stop-or-you'll-turn-into-a-cookie type of cookies.

She was thinking that Mici was right. The type of music she listened to on a regular basis, and the type she danced to, was at two different ends of the music spectrum. It was hard trying to choreograph a dance routine to anything by Bush. She'd tried, but the beat had either been too slow or too frenzied. She had no idea what kind of music Jarek liked. They'd never gotten around to discussing that yesterday. They'd been too engrossed in doing the lifts. She'd seen first hand that he could dance to Top Forty, but was that what he listened to all the time? *Guess I'll find out this afternoon,* she thought, absently biting into a cookie.

The warning bell rang, interrupting her thoughts. Glancing down at her hands, she noticed the crumpled ball of cellophane. She'd eaten the whole bag of cookies, give or take the two her friends had stolen.

"I really need to stop thinking so much," she mumbled under her breath.

***

It was three-thirty in the afternoon and Mattie had commandeered a smaller dance room. Jarek had brought his portable boom box, which had both a CD player and a tape deck, and a small case of CDs.

"Well, this should be pretty easy, you think?" Mattie said.

"No doubt. I've never done a themed routine before. Actually, this whole process is new to me. I mean, someone else always picks the music," he explained.

Mattie nodded in agreement. "That's usually how it goes. Do you take classes?" she asked, thinking she should have asked that question before now.

"Yeah, but I go to another studio. It was before Liz started this place," he told her.

"So why haven't you switched?"

Jarek gave her a funny look before saying, "Because I like my teacher and I have friends there. Besides, I've been there for years."

"What's it called? Where's it at?" Mattie probed.

"Half-Steppin' off of Washington."

Mattie's eyebrows rose. "I've heard of that place. They have dancers that end up on Broadway, among other places."

"Yeah, they do. The teachers are incredible," Jarek agreed.

Mattie's brow furrowed in thought. "Rhythm Station dancers have competed against you guys before. They don't make you choreograph your own routines?" she asked.

"Well, yeah, but someone else has always chosen the music. Most of the time, I just choreograph the routine," he said with a shrug.

Jarek watched Mattie tilt her head to one side and grin softly. Her expression clearly read that he had surprised her somehow.

"Really? I mean you...actually make up the steps before you hear the music?"

"Yep."

"Huh. That's...interesting," she remarked absently, her gaze moving to a point beyond his left shoulder.

Jarek leaned back on his hands. "What's *that* supposed to mean?" he asked warily.

Mattie returned her gaze to him. "Nothing except what it means. I didn't intend for it to be sarcastic."

"Well, how do *you* do it?" he wanted to know.

"There's something you'll notice about me once you get to know me," she began.

Jarek leaned forward, clasping his hands over his folded legs. "Yeah? And what's that?" he asked in a low tone, his eyes never leaving her face.

"Music. I listen to it constantly. I hear a song and I envision myself dancing to it. That's how I work. The music plays and I just create," she explained in a soft tone.

Jarek watched her closely, hardly daring to breathe for fear he would miss something. He was positive he would've kicked himself black and blue if he'd missed this particular admission.

"Is that what you want to major in? Dance?" he asked, not wanting to talk just then but thinking that he needed to.

Mattie's smile came and went so quickly, he wasn't even really sure he had seen it.

"I'm not sure yet. Music, dance, maybe both. But I have...other options I need to consider first," she replied evasively.

Jarek was going to ask about those options when she came out of her mental fog with the blink of an eye, then slapped on an over-bright smile. *Okay, so maybe now wasn't a good time*, he thought. The door marked Private Life had been gently closed, but he was grateful for the little peek he'd been given.

"So, do you...have any ideas for *our* routine?"

"Tons," he assured with an easygoing grin.

"So, do you wanna choreograph and I'll do music?" she offered.

Jarek's smile slipped a fraction. "We're a team now, Mataya. Fifty-fifty. I have ideas, sure, but I want your input, too. I know you choreograph your own stuff, so if you have any ideas, I'd like to see them," he stated sincerely.

Mattie beamed widely then slapped her hands on her knees. "Well, when I hear potential tunes, I make a Collage CD."

One corner of Jarek's mouth kicked up. "A Collage CD? What's that?"

"It's a recording of each song choice, but only like the first few minutes. Helps me narrow it down to one song, y'know? Anyway, I brought the original CD's from where I collected them in case you wanted to hear the whole thing."

Mattie reached into her purse, pulled out the CD case, and handed it to him. Jarek took it from her and silently read the selections that were printed on the cover:

Forsaken – David Draiman "Queen of the Damned"

A View To A Kill – Duran Duran "James Bond Collection"

Body Crumbles – Dry Cell "Queen of the Damned"

Buffy The Vampire Slayer Theme – Nerf Herder

Forever May Not Be Long Enough – Live "The Mummy Returns"

Die Another Day – Madonna "Die Another Day"

Party Up (Up In Here) – DMX "Gone in Sixty Seconds"

Hold Me, Kiss Me, Kill Me, Thrill Me – U2 "Batman Forever"

Haunting Me – Stabbing Westward "The Faculty"

Disappear – Metallica "Mission Impossible 2"

Bailamos – Enrique Iglesias "Wild, Wild West"

Bring Me To Life – EvanEscence "Daredevil"

"Stabbing Westward, Metallica, Live. They're alternative, aren't they?" Jarek inquired.

"Mmm, yeah. They are."

"I take it you like alternative music." It wasn't a question.

Mattie wasn't about to lie. "I do, actually. It's what's on in my car most of the time."

"You don't like R&B or rap at all?" he asked, almost hopefully.

"I like to dance to R&B, but not rap," Mattie responded truthfully. "I don't listen to it a whole lot, either. Rap is getting to be ridiculous. They talk about the same things: material possessions, money, women, and violence. They're always cussing, probably because they couldn't think of anything else to say, and they're always sampling other people's music. Whatever happened to being an original? And don't get me started on R&B. All those groups, male and female, are starting to sound alike. I can never tell the difference anymore."

Eyes sparkling, Mattie held up a hand to stop whatever Jarek had been about to say. If he'd been about to say anything in the first place, that is. Which he hadn't, for he was enjoying Mattie's reaction too much. It was as if he'd opened Pandora's box.

"Don't get me wrong. I have nothing against that type of music. I dance to it all the time. At Rhythm Station, at the clubs, at school dances. But you won't find hardly any of that kind of music in my collection," she added, finally winding down.

Jarek bit his bottom lip, trying not to laugh, and glanced at the CD case again. "Got a little Spanish stuff in there, too, I noticed," he commented, referring to the Enrique song.

"Yeah, well," she shrugged sheepishly, realizing how high she'd gotten on her soapbox. "Marc Anthony may be the real deal but I like the sexiness of Enrique."

"Yeah? What about Ricky Martin?" Jarek asked, slyly.

"Too much flash and cockiness. I don't know why everyone makes a big deal about the way he shakes his butt. It doesn't do anything for *me*. Truth to tell, I don't think he dances that well. And hey, Enrique probably doesn't, either. I've never really seen him dance, but I sure wouldn't mind being in one of his videos," Mattie ended on a sigh.

"Hmm," he murmured, thinking that sigh had been telling.

Hell, the whole conversation had been enlightening. She hadn't been kidding, either. She loved her music and had opinions on everything. Their tastes were slightly different, but it wouldn't be a hindrance to the relationship. If they *had* a relationship, he quickly amended. He was still trying to work the friendship angle.

"So I guess your radio stations are…?"

"One-oh-three-point-nine, The Edge, and ninety-eight KUPD," she supplied. "What about you, Jay? What's *your* music taste?"

"Uh," Jarek paused, then let out a chuckle as he held up his CD cases. "R&B mostly, with a little bit of rap thrown in," he answered.

Mattie's eyes widened as she groaned inwardly. *Way to go, Mataya,* she scolded mentally. *One Thousand and One Ways to Alienate The Opposite Sex by Mataya Black Hawk will be in stores tomorrow morning. Be sure to get a copy and check out the chapter on trashing his choice of music.* Feeling the heat steal up her cheeks, Mattie braved a look at Jarek.

"I'm sorry, Jay. I should've kept my mouth shut," she apologized.

Green eyes sparkling with amusement, Jarek laughed, shook his head and held up one hand. "It's okay, Mattie. *Really.* It's cool. Not everyone has the same taste in music, thank God. Life would be pretty dull if that happened. I admit, though, I was a little bit surprised."

Mattie's eyebrows lifted and she tilted her head to one side. "Surprised? How so?"

"Well. Aunt Liz says that you told her you like to fall asleep to slow music. So I was thinking you were really into artists like Sarah MacLachlan and Tori Amos—"

"I am," she interjected.

"And that's cool. I like a bit of Sarah Mac, too. But then at the dance contest, you danced like a *Solid Gold* dancer."

Mattie eyes widened again and she burst out laughing. "Oh my God! I used to love that show!" she exclaimed.

"Me, too," he laughed. "Hosted by Marilyn McCoo—"

"—And Rex Smith. I liked it when he sang 'Eye of the Tiger' because he wore the tiger-striped tank top and black leather pants," she added, laughing even harder.

"I used to have a crush on that African-American dancer with the really long hair. I can't remember her name, though," Jarek confessed.

"I used to have a crush on Denny Terrio," Mattie admitted.

This time it was Jarek's turn to throw his head back and roar with laughter. "*Dance Fever.* Holy cow. I almost forgot about that one," he said, wiping tears of mirth from his eyes.

"*I* didn't. I've always wanted to be a contestant on that show," she said.

"Well, *Dance Jam* isn't exactly like *Dance Fever* or *Solid Gold*—"

"It's way better," Mattie inserted.

"—But you're a contestant," Jarek concluded with a smile.

Mattie returned the smile, looking directly at him. "Yes, I am," she murmured softly. "And I'm glad you're my partner, Jay. I don't think I'd feel comfortable dancing with anyone else."

And she realized it was true. She was comfortable with Jarek. She felt safe with him. Mattie hardly ever felt safe with the opposite sex. Well, except for-oh, you know where this is going. It wasn't going to be easy. No one outside the family knew her secret, not even her best friends. Maybe she was worrying over nothing. Maybe, despite Liz's words, Jarek wasn't interested in her in that way.

Mattie glanced up to find his green gaze on her. And was it just her imagination or had he moved closer? When he started to lean forward slightly, eyes now focusing on her mouth, Mattie got her answer. She cleared her throat loudly, clapped her hands together and glanced around the studio.

"Well, we'd better get started. I have homework to do," which was a lie, "and I'll need to let the wolves in," which wasn't a lie.

Jarek jerked his head back as if he'd been slapped and nervously cleared his own throat. He nodded, tapping the case against the palm of his other hand. After studying the list a moment longer, he opened the case and handed Mattie the CD.

"Pop that sucker in and let's see what comes to mind."

"But what about the CDs *you* brought?" Mattie asked.

"I don't have that many and the ones I do have are mostly R&B and rap artists."

Mattie frowned, feeling guilty. "Well, we should give your CD's equal listening time then. I don't totally dislike your type of music, Jay. I guess it just depends who's on the radio at the time. I shouldn't have said what I said," she said.

Jarek reached out and put a hand on her arm. "It's okay, Mattie. I don't feel slighted. There are enough choices on yours to choose from and I'm sure we'll find something," he assured her.

Mattie studied his face for a long moment and she was glad he didn't look away. "Are you sure?" she asked.

Jarek nodded once. "Positive."

Finally, she took her CD from him and put it in the deck.

***

Two and a half hours later, after listening to five songs in their entirety, Jarek finally decided on Duran Duran's "A View To A Kill." It had come down to that song and Evanescence's "Bring Me to Life". He'd never heard of the group before and had liked their sound, but he'd had more steps that would fit with the Duran Duran song.

It had been interesting to see the process Jarek went through to choose the music. Conversation had been few and far between, but that hadn't bothered her one bit. She had enjoyed the show Jarek had put on for her. He'd paced around the small studio as he'd listened to each song, head down, forehead creased in concentration. Every once in a while he would suddenly face the mirror and execute a few steps. After watching him do that for about twenty minutes, she could tell which song would be eliminated.

She knew he had chosen the Duran Duran song when he'd danced a series of steps during certain parts of the song. Of course, playing the song twice in a row, after playing the others only once (and sometimes not even all the way through), had been a dead giveaway. She could see the James Bond stance in some of the moves and knew he would have to have a toy gun as a prop. From what she could see, it was going to be a pretty cool routine and she couldn't wait to get started.

At the end of the session, Jarek walked Mattie to her car. Before getting into his, he called to her.

"Hey Mattie."

She pushed the button that rolled down the passenger side window.

"Yeah?"

"I'm glad you're my dance partner, too," he said. "See you tomorrow."

CHAPTER SEVEN

Tuesday

"**M**attie, you've been awfully quiet. Is something wrong?" Mici asked tentatively at lunch.

"Yeah, you've barely touched your cookies," Ren added.

"And you really love those cookies, *cherie*," Mici tagged on.

"I was just thinking, that's all," Mattie murmured, a slight pucker to her brow.

"You aren't worried about the Dance-Off, are you?" Ren inquired, trying to get her friend to open up.

Mattie waved a hand. "No, no, no. Jarek and I are starting the routine tonight. And I'm going to go to Capezio's after school to see if I can find an outfit suitable enough to-"

She stopped abruptly when she realized she'd been about to say 'suitable enough to cover my scars.'

Ren and Mici looked at her expectantly.

"Suitable enough to what, *mon ami*?" Mici urged.

"To...uh...to look like a James Bond girl to his James Bond," Mattie stammered. *Nice save there, girlio,* she commended mentally.

Ren's eyebrows winged upwards.

"So, you guys are doing the secret agent thing, huh? Sounds pretty cool," she said. "What did you guys pick?"

"I bet it's the instrumental one, *oui*?" Mici guessed. "All the James Bond movies have that same something-exciting-is-about-to-happen type of music."

Ren scoffed. "Okay, Frenchie, like, I don't *think* so. That's the boring part. There's always a theme song to those movies.

Really cool ones, if I remember right. So which one are y'all doin'?"

"Duran Duran's 'A View to a Kill'", Mattie answered.

Ren nodded in an all-knowing way.

"Ah yes. Vintage Bond. Roger Moore, Tanya Roberts, Grace Jones, and Christopher Walken. Good choice."

Mattie chuckled and shook her head.

"*Haoli,* vintage Bond is Sean Connery in *Dr. No.* Or Roger Moore in *Moonraker. A View to a Kill* was back in the Eighties."

"You're right. Still, I thought *Goldeneye* would've been your Bond choice," Ren claimed.

"Ooooh, Pierce was *c'est magnifique,*" Mici gushed, kissing her fingers like an Italian.

"That song was too slow. I wanted something more upbeat," Mattie explained. "Besides, I was trying to get away from using slow songs. I didn't want to take the chance of putting the judges to sleep."

"Point taken. So he's gonna wear a tuxedo, I take it?" Ren asked.

"You take it right."

"I bet he'll look good in a tux," Mici commented.

"I bet he'll look *great* in a tux," Ren amended.

I bet he'd look great in a garbage bag, Mattie thought, but she didn't dare voice it aloud.

A moment of silence descended while the girls munched on their food. Left to her own devices, Mattie once again pondered on what to wear. It would have to be flashy and sexy, of course. She would be portraying a Bond girl, after all. She couldn't get *too* flashy and sexy, she thought with a wistful sigh. Not with the jagged scars that crisscrossed her back and the one on her upper chest. Mattie glanced at her watch. Lunch would be over soon. As much as she was looking forward to the end of the school day, she dreaded the shopping trip ahead. She tried to get her mind off of it by jumping back into conversation.

"So, Rennie, what soundtrack did you and Jamie choose?"

"Mmm." Ren quickly swallowed a mouthful of juice, raising one finger in a "just a minute" gesture.

"I think we're going with one of the Austin Powers soundtracks."

Mattie laughed. "Is he gonna dress up like Austin Powers?"

"Minus the teeth, I think. Although that would be pretty hilarious," Ren agreed with a laugh of her own.

"A Seventies costume shouldn't be that hard to find, *cherie*," Mici said.

"I know. I think I already have the go-go boots at home. Somewhere. Shoved way in the back of my closet," Ren joked, popping an orange section into her mouth.

"Do the guys at the skate-park know you're doing this contest thing?" Mattie asked.

Ren rolled her eyes and bounced her legs, making her wallet chain jingle.

"Oh, they tease and all, but I can tell they're impressed. It's like I'm representin' the crew, y'know?"

"Well, if you guys need to borrow a studio, Rhythm Station has a couple of empty ones for after hours use," Mattie offered.

"Thanks, but we got it covered. I told him I'd meet him at his dorm after school. He might even take me to dinner," Ren said with a sly smile and a waggle of eyebrows.

"You should watch yourself around those college boys, *mon ami*," Mici warned.

"I know how to handle myself. Thanks to Mattie, here."

The two girls exchanged high fives.

"Yeah, well, I gotta look out for my peeps," Mattie joked.

Mici reached up and tucked a strand of hair behind on ear.

"I did a reading last night," she announced suddenly.

Mattie and Ren paused to look at her face. She wasn't smiling.

"For who?" Mattie asked.

"The both of you."

Ren carefully set down her bottle of juice. "Why does that not sound good?"

"Because it's not. To make a long story short, there's a black cloud over this whole contest. Something just isn't right," Mici tried to explain.

"Is that why you didn't sign up with us?" Ren wanted to know.

"Partly. I mean really, the whole dance contest thing didn't appeal to me anyway. But I try to stay away from bad energy, and this whole contest practically *reeks* of bad energy," Mici proclaimed.

Mattie and Ren looked at each other, then back at Mici. They had never understood the charts and the tarot card readings, but she was good at it. *Really* good. Her predictions were rarely wrong. In fact, sometimes they were eerily right on target. Mattie glanced at Mici's wrists and noticed that she was wearing the beaded bracelet that repels negative energy. She was wearing them on both wrists and had a matching crystal around her neck. *Well, that definitely wasn't a good sign*, she thought. *Maybe I should be wearing those, too.*

Ren cleared her throat nervously and squirmed into a straighter sitting position.

"Should we be wearing one of those?" she voiced Mattie's exact thought, rubbing her own wrist.

Mici nodded. "*Oui*, you probably should. Both of you, really. I don't know why I didn't think of it sooner. I'll make a double stranded bracelet for you two tonight."

"Did you see anything specific about me and Ren?" Mattie asked, quietly.

"Nothing about Ren, but you had a strong presence. I think everything is going to be all right, though, *cherie*," Mici assured her, although she didn't sound so sure.

Mattie nodded and munched on her cookies. After hearing that, she could've eaten a whole box. Her friend's words cast a pall over the rest of the day, making it nearly impossible to concentrate in her last two classes. *It's a dance contest, for Heaven's sakes,* she kept thinking over and over. *What could possibly go wrong?*

***

The trill of a cell phone bounced off the walls and echoed ominously throughout the bathroom. The young man clenched his jaw and closed his eyes.

"Dude, you're phone's ringing," said a guy standing at the sink next to him.

"Tell me something I *don't* know," the young man murmured sarcastically.

"Better not be late, man. You know how anal the teacher gets," the guy said, ripping out a paper towel from the dispenser.

"Yeah, I know," the young man replied.

He waited until his classmate had left before answering the phone that hadn't stopped ringing. The caller didn't believe in leaving messages, so he knew he wasn't going to like the person on the other end.

"What do you want?" the young man demanded.

"That's no way to talk, Sonny," the voice said in a silky tone. "And you know what I want."

"I already gave you what you wanted," the young man shot back.

"Yes, well, did you happen to see the news the other night, Sonny-boy?"

"Stop calling me that. And yeah, I caught the news. So what?"

"Then you know it was slim pickings. We need healthy, not corroded."

"Look. I'm doing the best I can under the circumstances—"

"Do better," the voice interrupted. "We've got some needy clients, Sonny-boy. We need more...volunteers. You'd better find some more," the voice instructed.

"And what if I don't?" the young man taunted.

The laugh that came over the wire was so low and pure evil, the young man felt a shiver skim down his spine.

"Then you'll disappear, Sonny-boy. For good. Just do what you're told and you'll have nothing to worry about."

Click.

***

A half hour later found Mattie rifling through a rack of leotards, unitards and short filmy skirts at Capezio's. *Not too flashy, not too sexy, not too flashy, not too sexy, not too flashy, not too sexy,* she chanted mentally. She sighed, thinking about the kiss that almost happened. Jarek liked her or he wouldn't have tried it, but she wasn't sure how to respond. Despite the way she felt when she was with him, her first instinct was to keep him at a distance. Anyone who got too close was kept at arms length. Anyone who asked too many questions got pushed away altogether and ignored.

Tykota referred to it as her self-imposed exile. Her friends only knew so much about her and knew when to stop prying. When they had first asked about her parents, she'd told them they had died. Which was the truth, she just hadn't told them *how*. But being with Jarek, getting to know him, she was starting to rethink her exile. This was the first time she felt drawn to the opposite sex. For the first time, she was tempted to just...let go. To let somebody in and finally share the secret that weighed her down like a wet blanket. Why now? Why Jarek? Why not with Ren and Mici?

Mattie shook her head, not wanting to analyze it at the moment. She was looking forward to seeing Jarek today and they needed to concentrate on the dance routine. She didn't want to ruin the good feelings by being introspective. There would be time enough for that—WOW! She'd found it. She'd found the perfect outfit. Whipping the hanger off the rack, Mattie held it out in front of her. She checked the tag and saw that it was her size. She took it to the dressing room and decided to try it on. The dress was fire engine red, a color she knew emphasized her dark skin tone and pale blue eyes. The long-sleeved lace bodice flared to a filmy, chiffon, bi-level cut skirt that fell to mid-thigh. It was risqué enough for the look she was going for, yet it wouldn't earn a warning scowl from Ty. But the most important factor was it concealed what she was trying to hide.

Carefully taking it off, Mattie hung it back on the hanger. She climbed back into her own clothes, never once looking in the mirror. She never did that unless she was fully clothed. She wasn't crazy enough to wear high heels, although it would've looked better. But the floor might be slippery and it wouldn't do her any good to break a leg, literally, on local television. So she settled for a pair of matching red jazz shoes and took her purchases to the counter.

As she was walking to her Jeep, Mattie let out a startled sound as she glanced at her watch. Looking for her outfit had taken up a lot more time than she had thought. She was going to be late. She hurriedly jumped into her car and sped away.

"Sorry I'm late," Mattie breathed huffily as she rushed into the studio.

Jarek was sitting on the floor, legs stretched out, upper body bent forward. He straightened up when he'd heard the door open.

"You're not too late. I just got here a few minutes ago myself," he said by way of greeting.

"Oh good," she sighed in relief. "I went shopping for my outfit after school. I didn't think it would take that long," she explained.

Jarek beamed a bright smile. *Good God, why did I leave my sunglasses in the car?* Mattie thought. *Is it possible to go blind from being exposed to a smile?*

"Really? I was, too. Getting fitted for a tux, I mean. Well, the jacket and shirt anyway. I'd probably rip the pants with all the jumping around we'll be doing," he joked.

"I see what you mean. But do you think you'll be able to dance in a tux jacket?" Mattie asked, joining him on the floor to warm up.

As she stretched a leg to one side and folded the other in front of her, she surreptitiously checked him out. He was wearing a white tank top and navy blue workout pants. Her gaze strayed to his upper body. The tank top looked well worn in places, but still managed to hug his pecs-Mattie swallowed-quite nicely.

"...Taking it off," Jarek was saying.

"*What?*" Mattie squawked, popping up straight. Had she unknowingly said something aloud?

Jarek looked at her and blinked once. *What did I say?*

"What did you say?" Mattie voiced aloud.

"I said that I would be taking it off. The tux jacket?" he repeated. "You had asked me if I would be able to dance with it on."

"Oh, uh, oh. Right," she stammered. *Idiot.*

Feeling the heat steal up her cheeks, she changed positions so she was bending over in the opposite direction.

"Yeah, I got this idea. I went home and burned the music at the beginning of a James Bond movie onto a CD. Y'know, that part where he walks on screen, then faces the camera with the little gun in his hand?" he began to explain.

Before Mattie could comment, he went on.

"Classic scene. Anyway, at that point I thought you could walk up, take the jacket off, and toss it somewhere. Or throw it over your shoulder and toss it aside later. I dunno. I haven't figured that part out yet. But that could be our beginning pose before the actual music starts." Jarek shrugged. "It was just an idea."

"But it's a great one. I like it. I didn't even think about using that scene. And you're right, it *is* a classic," Mattie agreed.

"It's funny, I never would've thought of it myself had I not seen the clip. TBS is doing their Bond Marathon thing again and I ended up watching *Moonraker* last night," Jarek said.

"I'm not a Roger Moore fan, but that was my favorite out of all of his," Mattie retorted.

"So, you're a James Bond fan?" he inquired.

"Who isn't? But I prefer Sean and Pierce. I like that one of Roger's and Timothy Dalton in *The Living Daylights*. I didn't care for him too much in *License to Kill*, though" she replied.

"Uh-huh," Jarek murmured. *I'll have to keep that in mind,* he thought.

"So, shall we get started?" Mattie asked, slapping her hands on her legs.

Two and a half hours later, Mattie and Jarek were getting tired and it was starting to show. During one of the lifts, his foot slipped and they'd both gone down. Mattie's instincts had kicked in and she'd been able to keep herself from getting hurt by going with the momentum of the fall. She curled herself into a ball and somersaulted out of it onto her back, making sure her weight was centered on her feet. She lay there on her back for a moment, trying to catch her breath. She knew that trick would come in handy someday. Mattie didn't know how many times she and Tykota had practiced that move, but she'd finally been able to use it. *He would be proud,* she thought on a tired sigh.

The next thing she knew, Jarek was leaning over her, concern and fear etched in his features, words tumbling out of his mouth.

"Holy shit. Mattie, are you all right? Are you hurt? Talk to me. Wait, don't move," he put his hands on her shoulders to stop her movements.

"Jay—"

"I'm so sorry, Mattie. You have to believe that I would *never* let you fall—"

"Jay," she tried again, to no avail.

"It's just that my foot slipped. I couldn't control it and the next thing I knew—"

"Jarek." Mattie was up on her elbows, practically nose to nose with him. She realized her mistake too late. He was closer than she thought, for he hadn't moved back to give her space. His attention had gone from checking her for bodily injuries to focusing solely on her mouth.

"Yeah?" he said huskily, his body utterly still. His gaze flickered between her eyes and her mouth.

Mattie remained in her position, afraid to move, afraid to breathe. Her elbows would get sore pretty soon, so she knew she wouldn't be able to hold the position for very long. She cleared her throat nervously and spared him a quick glance.

"I'm all right," she managed to get out.

"Oh. Good," he murmured, leaning a fraction closer. "I was worried that I'd have to call 9-1-1 or something."

His last words were a feathery breeze across her lips before he brushed his own lips over them. He lifted his head a little bit after the first pass, waiting, watching. He raised an eyebrow, a silent question.

Mattie knew he was expecting a response. Hopefully not a verbal one, because she couldn't have spoken a coherent word at the moment if her life depended on it. She glanced at his mouth, then stared deeply into his clear green eyes. Actually, they weren't as clear as they usually were, but closer to the color of the tall grass at her house. And he never looked away, not once. She nodded her head imperceptibly.

Jarek's body relaxed—had he been holding his breath?—as he reached up to run the back of his fingers down her cheek. He laced one arm around her waist and the other over her shoulder and down her back, lifting her up to cradle her against his chest. He leaned back until he was sitting, one leg pulled up so her back was propped against it. He ran both hands over her head where they cupped the back, and leaned down to kiss her once again.

Over and over his lips brushed, nipped, nibbled and clung, never taking more than was offered. Soft and tender kisses were dropped on her forehead, nose, and cheeks before Jarek moved back to her mouth. Mattie's sense of safety was once again reinforced when his hands remained cradling her head. They were splayed, so at intermittent moments, she would feel a caress near her ear or mouth. With one last brush of his mouth over hers, Jarek lifted his head to look down at her.

"Are you sure you're all right?" he asked huskily, outlining her eyes with an index finger.

"I'm fine. Totally....fantastic," Mattie responded dreamily, her eyes never leaving his face.Jarek smiled and lightly pinched her cheek. "We should probably get going. I think we've practiced enough. Besides, I think I could perform our routine in my sleep," he said.

"Yeah, me too. And I know I'll be sore," Mattie agreed.

"Are you hungry? Did you wanna grab something to eat?" Jarek asked, helping her to stand.

He stood up next to her and they automatically did a few cooling down exercises.

"Oh, no. That's okay. Ty will have something light made for me by now, I'm pretty sure," Mattie replied.

Jarek strode to the wall and snatched up his duffel bag. "This is the second time you've mentioned this guy. Is he your father?" he asked in what he hoped was a casual tone.

It seemed that nothing got past her. She was hyper-aware of everything that went on around her and she could probably sense when something wasn't right. Like a guy trying to hide his streak of jealousy and hoping he was successful.

"He's *like* a father, yes," Mattie answered cautiously.

That caught his attention. "But he's not your real father." It wasn't a question.

Mattie glanced at him, then away. "No. He's not my real father."

Jarek paused, waiting for her to elaborate. When nothing else was forthcoming, he decided to probe a little deeper.

"So, he's your guardian then?" he guessed.

Mattie tilted her head to the side as if thinking. "Yes. But I prefer to call him my Protector. With a capital P. That's the word his people use, so I use it, too. It sounds better and it fits him," she explained.

"His people?"

"Tykota is a full-blood Apache," Mattie stated.

Jarek's eyebrows rose. "Uh-huh. So what happened to your biological parents?"

Jarek had never seen someone shut down so fast. He could see it in her face and it was unsettling to watch. Her face went blank, almost slack, and her eyes turned an even icier blue if that was possible. Once again, the door marked Private Life had not only been closed, but slammed shut and locked with a dead bolt.

"This studio is going to be in use tomorrow, so why don't you come over to my house? I have enough space for us to practice," Mattie said flatly, shouldering her duffel bag.

Jarek nodded, backing off for the moment. He didn't want her to push him away. He'd gotten another glimpse into her life, a glimpse she *really* didn't want to talk about. Had she been abandoned? Had her parents died in an accident? He was curious. Curious to let well enough alone for now. He would be seeing where she lived, possibly meeting the man she referred to as her Protector-with-a-capital-P. That will definitely be an enlightening experience.

"C'mon, I should lock up. I'll give you directions in the parking lot," Mattie said, heading for the door.

***

Driving home, Mattie replayed the scene in the studio over and over again. She'd let her guard down. She'd decided that she was going to let her guard down when she realized he was going to kiss her. And Yowza, what a kiss. But then he'd ruined the afterglow by asking about her parents. Obviously, that was still a sore subject with her and she wondered if it always would be. This secret she carried kept her from getting close to anyone. She didn't need a psychiatrist to tell her that. She would tell him, Mattie decided. She would tell him everything. After the dance contest.

When she pulled up into the cottage driveway, she was surprised to see a company Hummer parked near the front door. Mattie's heartbeat picked up as she realized it was probably Tykota's crew. She parked in the garage, jumped out and ran inside. This was unusual because the guys were usually on assignment. She dumped her backpack and duffel bag beside her desk, toed off her sneakers, and followed the sound of masculine voices. It was Tykota's buddies, all right. She paused in the shadows of the hallway and watched them for a moment.

Ramsey, Storm, Cole and Heath were Tykota's closest friends. During their six-year stint as Navy SEALs, he had been the captain of their Extraction Unit. When Tykota had come for her, they too had quit the military; No regrets, no looking back. Ramsey, her favorite of the group, had told her once that the guys hadn't wanted to be split up and placed elsewhere; nor had any of them wanted to take over as leader. He'd said that each man had had a specialty, and Tykota's had been captain; a natural leader. "It was the only logical choice. And it seemed like the right time to quit," he'd said.

Too true, Mattie couldn't help but think. She knew these five men had covered each other's backs during their missions. She knew they all would've died for one another. But how long before one of them, or *all* of them for that matter, died doing their job? Mattie often wondered if Tykota would still be a Navy SEAL if he hadn't found out about her. Probably. Maybe.

When Mattie had started high school, Tykota had quit Zion Security to start his own company, Black Hawk Protection

Agency: specializing in the personal protection of children ages four to nineteen. He'd done it because of her, she knew, and what had happened to her in the past. Who knew there were so many children that needed to be protected; and not just the children of royal families or famous actors, but ordinary children with ordinary lives? It was upsetting to Mattie that people would use children as pawns in their games to one up each other. And it upset her that Tykota's business, the majority of which was referrals from his former employer, was doing so well. It meant that there were children in danger. A *lot* of children.

But she was glad that Tykota had seen the need for such a business. Ramsey, Storm, Cole and Heath worked the international clientele, while Tykota continued to hire and train men for the domestic clients. He had been her Protector from the time she was seven and she considered herself lucky. But the other guys were just as good, if not better. Any child would feel lucky, and safe, to have any of them as a Protector.

Judah came up and nudged her into the light, making the men abruptly stop talking. Mattie watched in amused curiosity as they each transformed their expressions from serious intent to casual neutrality. *God, how do they do that?* She wondered, even as she went to hug each of them.

"I thought you guys would be on your next assignments by now," Mattie said, heading for the kitchen.

"We are," Ramsey called to her.

Mattie paused in the process of pulling down a glass. "Your assignment is here? In the valley?" she asked.

"Yep," this from Storm.

"But you and the guys do the international stuff," Mattie pointed out.

"This *will* be international. If it isn't already," Heath said in his deep baritone.

Before she knew it, all five men were in the kitchen with her. *You should be used to this by now*, she told herself with a hand over her thumping heart. *They all move like freakin' ninjas.*

"How was dance practice, sweetling?" Tykota asked in his soothing tone.

"Great. We chose the music today, a James Bond them, and cranked out a routine. I'll be sore, but it'll be worth it. I also bought an outfit after school. Very Bond girl-ish."

Mattie filled her glass with ice, then poured in bottled water all the way to the top. She tipped it up and emptied about half the glass before she realized they were still there, waiting quietly. She slowly lowered the glass, leaned against the counter and gazed at them. They hadn't moved an inch. The men had formed a half-circle around Tykota, legs spread apart, hands clasped in front of them. It was what Mattie referred to as their civilian "at ease" stance, but with the hands clasped in front instead of in back. *You can never really leave the military, can you?* She thought.

"Why do I have the feeling I'm not going to like your next assignment?" she asked ruefully.

"Probably because you are not, sweetling," Tykota said, "but you need to be made aware of the situation."

Mattie shifted and put the glass down. "What's going on?"

"Does the name John-Michael Carsten sound familiar to you?" Tykota asked.

Mattie tilted her head and ran the name mentally through her mind. Then she shook her head. "No. Do you have a picture?"

Cole handed her a black and white mug shot of a man with shoulder-length, scraggly black hair, bushy eyebrows and a bushy mustache that totally covered the man's mouth. Ew.

"He looks like a Mexican drug lord," she commented, handing the picture back.

A corner of Ramsey's mouth kicked up. "He's not."

"I don't recognize him. What has he done?"

Instead of answering the question, Tykota handed her another picture. This time, it was in color, a school picture. The girl had long blonde hair, brown eyes, and a friendly smile that revealed straight white teeth. She was a bit younger than Mattie, a freshman maybe? She felt her heart flip over in her chest.

"What's her name?"

"Cara Tyler. Do you recognize her?" Tykota inquired.

"No. Should I?"

"She goes to your school."

"A lot of kids go to my school, Ty. I don't know the majority of them."

"She is a sophomore."

"I'm a senior. And never the twain shall meet unless she's a genius. What's going on? Is she dead?" Mattie asked, practically throwing the picture back at him.

"No. A couple of days ago, she woke up with a fresh scar on her right side. Her kidney had been removed," Tykota began to explain.

Mattie's breath came out in a whoosh and she was thankful that the counter was at her back supporting her weight. She opened her mouth to say something, but the only thing that came out was a hoarse squeak of disbelief.

Seeing that he at least got a response, Tykota continued. "The only thing she remembers about the night before was dancing at a club called The Ozone. There were other victims, too, not all of them girls."

"But what does that have to do with me?" *Oh, good, Mattie. You finally found your voice,* she congratulated herself.

"They were all carrying the same evidence: a VIP Pass for *Dance Jam Productions.*"

CHAPTER EIGHT

Wednesday

I *will get through this day,* Mattie thought when her eyes opened the next morning. *I will get through this day. Everything will be all right. I'm too young to have a nervous breakdown.* She sighed, rubbed a hand across her forehead and closed her eyes again.

"Is it possible for a brain to explode from too much thinking?" she murmured aloud. "If so, I think it's about to happen."

What did Tykota expect her to do to with the information he'd told her yesterday? Tell Ren? Forfeit the contest? Ironically, later on that night, she'd watched the news. She'd caught it just in time to watch a reporter interview one of the victims: an eighteen-year-old male who was to be graduating from high school in just a few months.

He was from a big family, who couldn't afford to pay for their children's education, so he'd been planning to enlist. Those plans had been cruelly dashed when his kidney had been removed. The military did not accept recruits who have had major operations. And losing a kidney definitely qualified as such.

But Mattie couldn't think about that now. She had other things on her mind, as she always did around this same time every year. Today was the tenth anniversary of her family's death. Today, at three, she would go out to The Memory Tree and pay homage to the ones she'd lost. The Memory Tree was one of five sturdy oak trees in their huge backyard, but it had been planted on the very edge of the property. Five white crosses surrounded the base of the tree, one for each member of the Maikainai family: Iolani, her mother, Koa, her father, Kelecko, her older brother, and Neilani and Tabica, her brother's children.

She *would* get through this day, she vowed again. She had been doing the same thing for the past nine years. The first few visits had been difficult, but the pain had lessened year after year. As she'd grown older and learned the different methods of remembrance, the premise of her visits had changed. A CD with a mix of songs played on a boom box had replaced the traditional Mourning Dance that was usually performed on the island.

"I have made breakfast for you, sweetling."

The sound of Tykota's voice had both Mattie *and* Judah jumping in startled surprise. As if understanding the word food, Judah hopped down off the bed, stretched, and padded by Tykota, pausing for the usual scratch behind the ears. She sat up, pushing a hank of hair out of her face with another sigh.

"You do not have to do this today, you know," he said.

Mattie smiled sleepily at the familiar words. He'd been saying that same phrase for nine years. And her reply was always the same. "I know. But they're my family."

She no longer remembered their birthdays. The dates hadn't seemed important during that trying time. So the ceremony at The Memory Tree had been the next best thing. But today was going to be different.

"Come. Get dressed and we will start our lesson," Tykota invited. "I will be waiting for you in the studio," he added before turning away.

Mattie nodded, running both hands through her hair. She did it again, this time tucking it behind her ears. The third time, she pulled it to one side. Idly stroking the long strands, she stared into space as an idea began to form in her mind. Putting it aside for now, she tossed the covers aside and stood up. Yes, today was going to be different.

***

"So. You found an outfit, *cherie?"* Mici asked at lunch.

It was just the two of them today. Ren had left right before lunch to go to a doctor's appointment.

"Yeah. It's very pretty. It's not what I would usually wear, but it'll do for the contest," she replied.

"Yes, well, if you guys get chosen, you'll probably be wearing even less," Mici drawled with a quirked eyebrow.

That's what I'm afraid of, Mattie thought with slight discomfort. Aloud, she said, "We'll see."

"Has Jarek seen it yet?"

"Nuh-uh. Not 'til Friday. Although he *is* coming over tonight," Mattie said.

"Why do I get the feeling that Ty has no idea?" Mici countered.

"Probably because he doesn't," Mattie admitted guiltily. "I forgot to mention it this morning. I had other things on my mind."

Mici chuckled. "I wish I could be a fly on the wall when he comes over, *mon ami.* Ty can be quite intimidating."

"Tell me about it," Mattie muttered under her breath.

Taking her literally, Mici proceeded to do so.

"I remember the first time Ren and I came over to your house. When Ty opened the door, I felt like that little girl in *Annie* who kept saying 'Oh my goodness, oh my goodness'".

Mattie let out a bark of laughter and Mici joined her.

"I don't know if he would've carried me in if I'd fainted, though," Mici added, still laughing.

Mattie laughed even harder. "You were lucky that Dar and Judah were running around out back," she said around leftover chuckles.

"Jarek might not be so lucky. Ty reacted differently around us, y'know?" Mici pointed out.

Mattie's smile dimmed somewhat at that comment. "I hadn't thought of that," she voiced aloud.

"Ty's very protective of you, *cherie.* I mean, Ren and I are females, so he really has no reason to feel threatened, but..." Mici trailed off with a shrug.

"Jarek is another story," Mattie supplied with dawning clarity.

Mici nodded, taking a swallow from her bottled water. She glanced down at her sandwich, then over at Mattie.

"I watched the news last night, *mon ami,*" she announced quietly.

Poof! Mattie's appetite was gone in an instant.

"I did, too," she admitted.

"Did you see the segment about—"

"About the male victim who can't enlist now because of what happened?" Mattie interjected. "Yeah. I caught that."

"They're saying that the victims were dancers for the show," Mici pointed out.

Mattie stared at her friend for a moment. "No, not regulars. They just had the VIP Pass," she said.

"Like that makes any difference. Same club, same evidence. That's too much of a coincidence, don't you think?" Mici asked.

Mattie shook her head. She'd never heard her friend talk like this before.

"Mici, about that reading you did—"

"Do you think *Dance Jam* is involved somehow?" Mici interrupted.

"Ty seems to think there's a connection," Mattie answered cautiously.

"Oh..." Mici breathed, shaking her head. "This cannot be good if Ty is involved."

Mattie licked her lips. "A-and the guys are home," she admitted.

Mici's eyes practically bugged out of her head. "*All* of them?"

Mattie nodded.

"But they're international only."

Mattie said nothing, knowing it would click for her in a minute. Or two. Or three? Maybe fo—

"Mattie, I think you need to drop out of this contest. I did that reading for you, remember? I told you that you would be a part of this, but I did not think it would be this way," Mici said in disbelief.

"I can't just quit now. We've come this far—"

"I have to call Rennie. She will need to know this," Mici rushed on, her movements agitated.

"*What?* Are you out of your mind? She'd never agree to do th—"

"I brought the bracelets for both of you, but I don't think it will help. I should do another reading, *oui?* Just to be sure. Maybe I was wrong. Maybe I read the cards wrong the first time and—"

"Michelle," Mattie practically shouted, making her friend jump. "Do you hear yourself? You seriously need to calm down or you're going to be speaking French soon."

Mattie didn't understand it. Mici was always the calm one. You'd never know it by looking at her right now though. She was so fidgety you'd think she'd had a mocha latte with ten shots of espresso.

"You and Ren with those accents," Mattie scoffed, shaking her head. "I swear, you two are a trip and a half."

Mattie watched her best friend pull herself together. She patted her cap of red curls, adjusted her glasses and smoothed her long skirt over her knees. Pieces of jewelry chimed and rattled, and Mattie wondered if any of those gemstones invoked inner calm. Maybe she'd forgotten to wear that one today.

"You know Rennie won't quit, Mic. She's gotten this far, gotten a chance to meet Chris. There's no way. *Dance Jam* is her favorite show. If she had a chance to be a regular on the show, do you think she'd just quit? I don't think so. Ty and the guys will find out what's going on before Friday and she'll never have to know," Mattie reassured her.

Mici nodded even though it didn't look like she believed her. Mattie didn't quite believe it much herself. But she believed in Tykota, and his friends, and their ability to do their job. She knew that he would never let anything bad happen to her. Not ever again.

***

The moment she got home, Mattie went straight to her room and prepared herself for the ceremony. She dressed herself in an ankle-length sarong skirt and a half top that left one shoulder and her torso bare. She then slipped a bracelet made of white hibiscus flowers around her left ankle, the leg that was exposed due to the thigh high slit in the skirt. The whole ensemble, white hibiscus flowers on a red background, was nothing like what was usually worn on the island, but it was close enough. It had seemed an appropriate tribute to her family, who'd been buried on the island, and it reminded her of the home she'd left behind.

CELISE DOWNS

Moving to her make-up table, she sat down in front of the mirror, pulled her hair over one shoulder and began to brush it. Her movements became slow and hypnotic as she studied her image in the mirror. The top aptly covered the one jagged scar on her chest, only two inches of it showing above the fabric. If she turned around, however, the view would be different. Mattie blinked, and suddenly, Tykota was behind her, taking over the task of brushing her hair. He looked at her in the mirror.

"It is almost three o'clock, sweetling," he told her.

She gave him a serene smile. "I know."

He concentrated on brushing her hair for a few moments, before once again catching her eyes in the mirror. "You seem at peace today. More so than you have in the past couple of years," he commented.

Mattie sighed softly and crossed her legs. "I am."

Tykota nodded once, saying nothing else.

"I heard another voice. Is one of the guys here?" Mattie asked.

Tykota smiled as he picked up the white hibiscus flower lying on the table. "Ram," he answered.

"Ah. Well, I'm expecting company tonight. Jarek is coming over so we can go over the routine." She paused to give him a warning look. "So please leave your intimidation mask in a box and Dar in another room."

"As you wish," he murmured, tucking her hair behind her right ear and securing it with the flower.

Tykota stood behind her, hands cupping her shoulders, gazing intently at her image. A moment later, he squeezed her shoulders and was about to step away when Mattie clamped her hand over one of his. She blinked rapidly and swallowed convulsively, trying to get past the sudden lump in her throat.

"I love you, Tykota Black Hawk," she whispered in his native tongue, her eyes clinging to his in the mirror.

"I love you, too, Mataya Black Hawk," he returned.

He squeezed her shoulders again and walked out. Returning her gaze to her reflection, Mattie inhaled deeply, exhaled slowly, then straightened her shoulders. She stood, picking up her boom box and the photo album as she did so. She walked out the back door of her room, the one that led to the backyard, and made her way to the edge of the property. Minutes later, Judah padded into step beside her as she made her trek to the Memory Tree.

At approximately three o'clock Mattie opened the CD case and examined the list of songs she played every year.

The Rose – Bette Midler (Mother)

Moon River – Unknown (Father)

I Bid You Goodnight – Aaron Neville (Brother)

Hakuna Matata – Lion King Soundtrack (Children)

It's So Hard To Say Goodbye To Yesterday – Boys II Men (Whole Family)

She put the CD in the deck and pushed Play. As the piano intro to "The Rose" began, Mattie opened the photo album. It wasn't long before the memories came flooding back. The pain wasn't as strong as it had once been. She could remember a time during the first few years of paying homage, when she hadn't been able to get through the whole album without sobbing uncontrollably. Now, as the song shifted to "Moon River", a lump lodged itself in her throat and wouldn't budge no matter *how* many times she swallowed.

She was able to release a small smile, however, as she flipped through the pictures of her older brother. At the age of seven, Mattie had known her brother was handsome and popular with the girls. They'd called the house all the time. Despite the fact that Kelecko been ten years older, they'd still been close. He'd always had time for his little sister. He had been the spitting image of their father with his dark wavy hair, warm brown eyes, and teasing smile. Every time she looked at Tykota, it was a constant reminder of what kind of man Kel would've become if he'd lived. He and Kel had been best friends once, sharing the same interests as well as the same age.

Mattie turned the page, lovingly caressed a school picture, and mouthed the words as Aaron Neville sang. "'Lay down my dear brother, lay down and take your rest. I want to lay your head upon our Savior's breast. I love you, but Jesus loves you best. I bid you goodnight, goodnight, goodnight'." She closed the album altogether when the next song came on, smiling as she hopped onto the rope swing Tykota had made for her. She knew the kids would've loved this song, not to mention the movie.

"Hakuna Matata, what a wonderful phrase'," she sang to Judah as she swung by him. "'Hakuna Matata, ain't no passin' craze. It means no worries, for the rest of your days. It's our problem free…philosophy. Hakuna Matata'".

Grasping the rope with both hands and leaning back, Mattie swung crazily to and fro, back and forth, as she sang loudly with Timon and Pumbaa. The swinging and the singing dwindled considerably when the song ended and Boys II Men started.

"No more worries, guys," she whispered to the smaller crosses signifying her niece and nephew. "No more worries."

She stopped pumping, letting the swing glide on its own. Mattie leaned her head against her hands, closed her eyes and just let the words wash over her. "'If we get to see tomorrow, I hope it's worth all the pain. It's so hard to say goodbye to yesterdayyyyyeeee'".

When the song ended and the boom box shut off automatically, Mattie slowly climbed off the swing and kneeled down in front of her parents' crosses. She had to clear her throat twice, swallow three times, and blink rapidly *several* times before she was able to speak.

"Y'know, I've played that song for you guys three years in a row and I've never taken the words to heart until now. For...so long, there was so much anger inside me, so much guilt. And I couldn't, *wouldn't*, let go of that day no matter what Tykota said," Mattie paused, glancing at the other crosses.

"Ten years. Ten years of visiting you guys, talking to you guys, playing music for you. But things have to change. *I* have to change. I have to stop living in yesterday and move on to tomorrow. I know you all would want me to do that."

Mattie stopped, pressing trembling fingertips to her mouth. She blinked and tears spilled down her cheeks. Sniffing loudly, she wiped them away with the heel of one hand. Judah moved to her side, offering silent comfort. Slipping an arm around his bulky body, she leaned her head against his neck.

"I love you all and that's something that will *never* change. But Ty is my family now and you'll be happy to know that he's doing a wonderful job of raising me. He made sure that..."

Mattie's features contorted as she tried to search for the right word. She knew the word she *wanted* to use, but she was in the presence of children, after all.

"...That pitiful excuse of a human being that took you all away from me will never hurt anyone ever again. And I have to be happy with that, because no matter how hard I wish, I can't bring you all back. I just hope that wherever you all may be, that you're all together, and happy, and safe, and that you're no longer...in pain."

The sob escaped before Mattie could stop it and she buried her face in Judah's fur to muffle the ones that followed. She didn't know how long she cried. What seemed like hours were probably just mere minutes. But her chest no longer felt tight and the muscles in her shoulder blades relaxed. The burden had been lifted. After ten long years, she'd finally let go. Sitting on her legs, she placed her hands on her knees, closed her eyes, and raised her head.

"Dear Lord, please watch over my family. Let them know how much I love them and how I wish I could be with them. M-make sure the scars don't show too badly. My Mama always had beautiful skin. A-and Kel's smile could always charm the coconuts from the trees. The twins get into mischief every once in a while, but I'm sure you know that already. But they're good kids all the same. Just, uh, make sure their...little outfits don't get too dirty and their wings don't get caught in any doors.

I-I'm trying to understand why my family was...sent to you. Why they're with you and I'm still here. I suppose I'll always wonder about that. But you brought me Ty and I will always be grateful for his presence. He's taught me well, as you know, and I'll try not to let him down. I also wanted to thank you for Renee and Michelle...and Jarek. Blessings in disguise, I'm sure. I'm not angry anymore. At me, at you, at the man who took my family. I think I've given it all up to you. I think I'm at peace now, *really* at peace. So my family can rest in peace in now, too. If their spirits still linger here because of me, you can take them home now. In Christ's name, amen."

After making the sign of the cross, Mattie got to her feet, picked up her boom box, and laid a hand on her companion's head.

"Come, Judah. Time to go back."

Going to her room, Mattie quickly took off her outfit and took a shower, leaving her hair damp.

"Computer, locate Tykota," she instructed, pulling on black yoga pants and matching spandex top.

"Compliance. Tykota is in the weight room," the computer intoned.

"Ty, can you c'mere a minute, please?" she requested, pulling a ratty T-shirt from her chest of drawers.

Moments later, he silently appeared in her doorway, his shorts-clad body bathed in a sheen of sweat.

"Yes, sweetling?" he asked with a raised eyebrow.

Mattie reached for a pair of scissors on her dressing table and handed them to him.

"Cut it off to my shoulders," she said, then sat down in the chair.

A half hour later, Mattie closed the curtains in the studio, and turned on a light that shown dimly. She moved to the CD player and slipped Enya's "Watermark" album inside. She had some time yet before Jarek arrived and decided to do Tai Chi to clear her mind. Mattie pulled off the T-shirt and threw it down next to the CD player before strolling to the middle of the wooden floor. She gracefully sat down and began her warm-up exercises. She smiled when she noticed Judah slink in and settle in the shadows just to one side of the doorway. He'd started joining her in the studio last year, if the music wasn't too loud and there wasn't a lot of stomping going on. She didn't mind the company and he always alerted her when they were no longer alone. Of course, he did nothing but look up when Tykota or one of his friends peeked in, so she was surprised when he growled low in his throat an hour later.

"Oh my God," came a strangled voice.

Mattie, who had been in a stationary position, jerked her head up, looked in the mirror, and froze.

CHAPTER NINE

Wednesday/Secret Discovered

She stared at Jarek in horror, too stunned to move. Out of the corner of her eye, she saw the T-shirt she had tossed on the floor beside the CD player. The T-shirt that she would've been wearing by the time he had arrived. But it was too late. By the sound of his voice, she knew he'd seen what she'd always kept covered: four jagged scars crisscrossing her back.

"You're early," she tried for nonchalance.

"Mattie—" he took a step into the room, but froze when he heard the growling.

"Don't move," she warned.

Jarek released a nervous laugh. "You're going to have to use dynamite to get me to do that."

"Lights up," she said.

The fluorescent lights flickered on, forcing Jarek, Mattie, and even the wolf, to blink at the sudden brightness.

"Oh my God, Mattie," Jarek said again, his voice anguished now.

Under the harsh lighting, her scars appeared more garish. *Maybe that's why I keep it so dim in here*, she thought absently. She quickly strode over to the CD player and pulled on her T-shirt, not that it would do much good now. The damage had been done.

"Mattie—"

"Judah, come," she interrupted him with the sudden command.

He immediately left his post, his eyes never leaving Jarek as he moved towards her. He took his time, glancing at her to pinpoint her location. He came to a direct standstill a few feet in front of her, his back to her.

"Judah, come. Judah, sit," she commanded softly.

The wolf scooched back until Mattie was able to rest her hand on his head.

"Good boy," she praised in a low tone. "Good boy." She looked over at Jarek. "Set your backpack by the door," she instructed.

Jarek did as he was told, instinctively making his movements slow.

"Now what?" he asked after straightening up.

"Walk towards me. Slowly. Keep your hands away from your sides and whatever you do, don't look him in the eye," she instructed.

As he began to step towards her, Mattie proceeded to explain. "The object is to let him know you're a friend, not an enemy. He needs to know that you won't hurt me. Don't make any sudden movements and talk normally. Wolves can sense fear, smell it. And when they do, they use it against you."

Jarek nodded slowly in understanding, calm green eyes flicking between Mattie and the big animal at her side. He wasn't afraid. Not really. All he wanted to know was how she'd gotten those scars on her back. Who had done that to her? He wanted to ask, but couldn't quite get up the nerve yet. She was nervous. And she had every right to be, because he wasn't about to pretend he hadn't seen anything just because she'd put her T-shirt on.

"I thought you were joking about the wolf thing," he said in what he hoped was a normal tone.

"Why would I joke about something like that?" she asked in a flat tone.

He was about to shrug, then decided against it. "Because not too many people have tame wolves—"

"Ah, well, that's where you're wrong, Jay," Mattie interjected. "Judah's only semi-tame."

"Okay, fine," he conceded. "Not too many people have semi-tame wolves as house pets. You were smiling, cheekily I might add, when you mentioned it, so I thought you were joking. Or maybe..." he trailed off momentarily, reaching out and clasping the hand she had stretched out.

"Or maybe it's because you didn't want me asking anything personal, so you tried to throw me off," he completed in a whisper near her ear.

Mattie refrained from saying anything, just squeezed his hand and pulled him down to a kneeling position in front of Judah, who hadn't moved a muscle.

"Judah, this is Jarek. Jarek is a friend. Friend, Judah, friend," she said in a low soothing tone, holding their clasped hands under the wolf's nose. She spoke in Tykota's native tongue, for it was the only language he and his brother understood.

Judah sniffed the clasped hands then moved closer to Jarek. Mattie slowly released his hand and moved a few inches away. She watched as the wolf familiarized itself with Jarek's scent, toenails clicking as he circled him. When he went back to Mattie and pressed his forehead against hers, she smiled and leaned into the gesture. Jarek suddenly found himself jealous of a wolf.

"Does that mean I passed the test?" he teased, grinning at the affectionate scene.

It was comforting to know that she had such an alert protector in this animal she so obviously loved. Not to mention the man who'd greeted him at the front door. Yet where had her protectors been when she'd been inflicted with those scars?

"Yep, sure does. Jay, this is Judah Earl," she said, ruffling the fur at his neck.

"Judah Earl, huh?" he repeated, briskly scrubbing the wolf's back. "He's beautiful, Mattie. Really beautiful."

"Yes, he is," she agreed.

"What were you telling him?"

"That you were a friend."

"I figured as much, even though I didn't understand a word."

"Tykota is an Apache Indian. When Judah and his brother, Dar, were brought to him, he left them with his family for about a month. When he finally brought them home, not as wild and somewhat trained, they would only respond to the language of his people," Mattie explained, then shrugged. "I didn't want to mess with that. They were used to hearing it and I've been speaking the language for a long time anyway."

"So, he has a brother, huh?" Jarek asked, glancing around warily.

He didn't think he could withstand the trauma of going through another initiation ceremony.

"Yeah, Dar Magnus. But you won't meet him now. When Ty is home, he likes to stay close to him," she said.

"I feel honored seeing Judah up close and personal. I've always seen wolves on television. I was just thinking that they're a lot bigger in real life."

Jarek could hear himself talking, feel himself petting the wolf, but it seemed like he was watching through someone else's eyes. He was talking in a normal tone, but it didn't feel normal to him. He knew that Mattie was trying to distract him, hoping that he would forget? Not likely. His mind was telling him to confront her, yet his heart urged him to leave it alone.

But he knew it was impossible. He was beginning to have feelings for Mattie. More than friends type of feelings. Even if they ended up as nothing more, he couldn't ignore something as horrible as those scars. No matter how much she obviously didn't want to talk about it. Standing up alongside Mattie, they watched as Judah went back to his post by the door.

"He's your protector." It wasn't a question.

"Yes."

"Then what do you call that man who so kindly let me in?"

Mattie frowned. "Tykota didn't introduce himself?"

"Oh yeah, he did. I was just wondering what you call him," Jarek said with a shrug.

Mattie elicited a short chuckle, not sure where he was going with that comment. "Just Ty."

"Not Father or Dad?"

"He's not my father. He's my Protector."

Jarek nodded and said nothing, just watched her. And hoped. He wasn't going to ask the question that had been on the tip of his tongue. A question that hung in the air like an awkward moment. He hoped that she wouldn't shut him out and go on as though nothing unusual had happened. He watched the struggle go on inside her, a struggle that showed clearly on her face.

Her forehead bore a deep frown, troubled indecision filled her pale blue eyes as she stared at Judah, and she rubbed her hands together as though she were cold. Suddenly, she released a heavy sigh, closed her eyes, put her hands on her hips, and bowed her head.

"You want to know about the scars," she stated.

"I was kinda hoping we could talk about that," he said quietly. Tucking an index finger under her chin, he lifted her face until he could look into her eyes. Beautiful pale eyes that peered into a person's very soul.

"Mattie, I like you, as if you haven't noticed. I really like you a lot. And I would be a pretty insensitive guy if I didn't question what I saw. I can't just go about my business, practice this routine with you, and not wonder what happened. And I have a feeling you wouldn't be able to concentrate knowing what I know, always wondering when the other shoe would drop," he observed with a raised eyebrow.

"Possibly," she admitted after a short pause.

"And deep down you'd be disappointed that I didn't ask," he continued, stroking her lower lip with his finger.

Mattie swallowed. "Way...deep...down, I would imagine," she whispered.

Jarek leaned down and pressed his lips gently against hers. Lifting his head seconds later, he drew back to look down at her. When she leaned towards him, he kissed her again, deeper this time. He wrapped his arms around her, drawing her closer to him, and changed the angle of his head. Mattie hooked her arms under his and grasped his shoulders with her hands, hoping she wouldn't melt into a puddle at his feet. *But what a way to go,* she thought on a blissful sigh.

Bringing his hands around to cup her face, Jarek kissed her once more before lifting his head.

"I've wanted to do that again since yesterday," he whispered, then pressed a kiss to the corner of her mouth.

"Well, I suppose deep down I was hoping you would kiss me again, too," Mattie admitted with a short laugh.

Jarek smoothed both hands over her head before cupping her face again. "Tell me what happened, Mattie," he pleaded, staring deeply into her eyes.

She was shaking her head before he'd even finished the sentence. "You don't want to hear this, Jay. Really, you don't."

"I wouldn't have brought it up if I didn't," he countered.

Mattie removed her arms from around his back and began to pace around the studio. Taking a deep breath, she began to talk.

"I was born on the island of Maui in the little province of Kahului. I was seven and living on the island when it happened.

I remember coming home from school that day, sometime between three and three-thirty, opening the door, and smelling death," she paused and wrinkled her nose. Even after all this time she could still smell that horrible stench.

"I went to the kitchen, because that's where I always went I get home, and I found my mother lying in a pool of blood. God, it was everywhere, like something had leaked. The back door leading out to our backyard was open and I could see my father and older brother. They were dead, too, of course. They were near the door, so I knew they had been trying to help my mother."

"Oh God," Jarek choked out in a strangled whisper.

"I heard a baby crying. Hysterically crying—"

"Mattie—"

Jarek didn't want her to go on. He didn't want to hear anymore, but she wasn't listening to him. It was like she was in some kind of trance and he couldn't get through to her.

"—And I was thinking that I'd better go see what was wrong. The smell was even worse towards the back. The...man was still there. In our house. Neilani was already dead. He had already killed her. I stood there in the doorway and watched him kill Tabica. That's when I started screaming. I couldn't seem to stop screaming..." her voice trailed off as she stared into space.

Jarek was becoming alarmed. He was berating himself for even bringing up the subject. He wished that he had come at the appointed time. He wished that he had never seen the scars.

"Mattie, stop. You don't have to tell me anymore," he said, the words coming out in a nervous rush.

Mattie looked at him, but he had a feeling she wasn't really *seeing* him. "You asked, Jarek. You wanted to know, said it would be insensitive of you not to question what you had seen," she proclaimed in a soft voice, repeating his earlier words to the letter.

"I know, but I don't think I can take anymore—"

"If you don't let me finish now, I'll never talk about it again," she warned. "And I guarantee that you won't get anything out of Ty."

Jarek crossed his arms over his chest, bowed his head, and shifted his weight to one leg. After what seemed like hours, but was only minutes, he lifted his head and pinned her with an anguished gaze. It was harder on him than it was on her, she realized. She'd had to tell the story over and over again so much back then, that she had been able to find a place in her mind to shield herself. But it still got to her.

"Go on." The words felt ripped from his throat.

"He came after me with a knife. He got me in the back as I was running away, hence the scars. When he caught me…" her words halted.

Jarek clenched his teeth, blinked rapidly, and jutted his chin as though preparing for a blow.

Mattie tried again after clearing her throat and swallowing the lump the size of a tennis ball.

"When he caught me, he flipped me over and knifed my chest." She passed a hand over the front of her shirt.

She stopped pacing in the middle of the floor and stared at Jarek. Closing her eyes, she caressed the lids with her fingertips, tilted her head to one side, and crossed her arms as though she were hugging herself. Opening her eyes, she focused her gaze on Jarek again, who seemed to be frozen in place.

"My eyes were brown once, almost as dark as Ty's. I remember seeing the pictures," she said.

Jarek's head snapped back as if he'd received that blow he thought he'd been prepared to take. He could actually feel the blood drain from his face, and then fill back up again with barely leashed anger. God, how he wanted to hit something. Anything. He wanted to scream and shout...and hold Mattie and never let her go.

"He gouged out your eyes?" He could barely get the words out past lips that had grown stiff.

Mattie shrugged nonchalantly and paced to the glass wall that faced the backyard. She glanced over her shoulder at Judah, who was standing on all fours now and watching her like a hawk.

"He tried. Probably so I wouldn't be able to identify him. Or maybe he really did intend to kill me. Doesn't matter, anyway. It's not like I ever saw his face to begin with. He was wearing a ski mask," she said.

"Are your eyes transplants?" Jarek asked.

"Sort of," Mattie hedged.

Jarek frowned. "Meaning what? They're glass?"

Mattie snorted and rolled her eyes. "Do I look like a Marilyn Manson reject to you? The company Ty used to work for started branching out into areas beyond security," she began to explain.

"Areas like...?"

"Medical research. Skin grafting, cell regeneration, that kind of thing. My irises were reconstructed with a synthetic material similar to human flesh, then grafted into my eyeballs. It's just like any other grafting procedure. There's always a chance the new skin won't take..." she trailed off when Jarek suddenly came up and whipped her around.

He stared deeply into her eyes, trying to see the changes but knowing it wouldn't be possible. She'd done the same thing herself for almost six months after the surgery. Alone in her room, she would hold a mirror up to her face for hours, searching beyond the puffiness and the bruising. Nothing. After all was said and done, there had been no scarring, nothing visible to the naked eye.

He reached up and lightly touched the corner of her right eye with the tip of his index finger.

"And you can see perfectly?" Jarek asked in whispered awe.

"Twenty-twenty."

"Colors? Shapes?"

"Like a Picasso painting," Mattie replied with a smile.

"But...how is this possible? How could they possibly know...there are so many nerves in the eyeball that doctor's today still haven't found a way to replace an eyeball. I don't understand," Jarek said in confusion, still staring into her eyes.

Mattie's smile slowly faded. There was no easy way to break it to him. Taking a deep breath, she plunged in with both feet.

"It's not possible. Yet." *Okay, so maybe it was more like a toe-dipping than a plunge,* she thought with a wince.

Jarek's hand froze in the process of cupping her cheek. It was so quiet, she could hear Judah's shallow breathing as he sat by the door.

"What are you saying?" Jarek whispered.

"I-it was experimental. The material they used, the procedure. Everything. It was experimental. It wasn't approved by any health board," Mattie announced. And still wasn't, as far as she knew.

More dead silence. Then Jarek's mouth dropped open and his eyes widened in horror. "You were part of an *experiment*? An unapproved medical *experiment*?" he exploded.

Judah growled from the door, but Jarek paid no mind as he whirled away.

"They could've left you *blind*," he protested.

"I couldn't see in the first place," Mattie defended.

"You could've *died*," he ranted on.

"I didn't care," Mattie shot back.

Jarek faced her in stunned shock. *Had she meant to say that?*

Did I just say that? She asked mentally, gazing back at Jarek.

"That's not what you meant to say," Jarek said hoarsely.

Mattie sighed and shook her head. "Have I been talking out of my ass for the past half hour? Have you been listening to... *anything* I've just said? What—you think I've just been telling you about an article I read in a magazine or something? Let me break it down for you, Jay. I was seven years old and everything I had, everything that was *important* to me, had just been ripped away. I had nothing to live for. *Nothing.*

The whole time Ty was explaining the procedure to me, telling me what could or couldn't happen, the only thing I could think was 'I hope to God I die on the table'. Unfortunately, I didn't. So now I live with ugly, physical scars, nightmares, and freakish-colored eyes that I never wanted in the first place." *Okay, so maybe the nightmares occurred once or twice a year, but that was beside the point.*

"'I'm lucky to be alive', you say? Lucky? What's lucky? Lucky that I'm the only survivor of a family that's been brutally murdered? Boy howdy, that's luck all right. 'You should be happy', you say? I *would've* been happy if the guy had finished me off. But no, he was interrupted when a neighbor decided to drop by. Yeah buddy. I'll tell you what, my life is the bees knees right now."

Suddenly feeling drained, Mattie released a gusty sigh as she closed her eyes and pinched the bridge of her nose with her thumb and index finger. She walked over to the nearest wall and slid down until her feet were stretched out before her. Judah immediately trotted over to sprawl against her legs, putting his head in her lap.

"Look, you have to understand something. I didn't care about anything. I didn't want to live with the constant pain. Ty had me on suicide watch the first two years I was with him. He didn't dare leave me alone for fear I would kill myself. Smart man, cuz I would've tried the minute his back was turned. His friends would trade off watching over me. I got so used to the constant company that I started following Ty around the house. I didn't want to let him out of my sight for fear that I would never see him again. If he ever *did* leave the room, he made sure I knew where he was at all times by talking. Or making a lot of noise." Mattie chuckled at the memory. "You've met Ty. Making a lot of noise and talking a lot goes against his nature, not to mention his training. But he did it for me. He and the guys."

Mattie ran her hand over Judah's head and down his flanks in slow, hypnotic strokes. She knew the minute Jarek sat down next to her because Judah raised his head and growled.

"Hush now, boy," she crooned. "He means no harm. I was homeschooled until the eighth grade. Now that I think back on it, he probably kept me home for so long because he was afraid someone might try to kill me again. Maybe that I might try to do it myself even though I was showing signs of recovery. Even now, on occasion, he still likes to pick me up from school or work." Mattie sighed again, opened her eyes and turned her head to the right to look at Jarek.

"I imagine we're not going to run through the routine today. I know you have questions," she stated.

"Why aren't you staying with relatives?"

Mattie winced inwardly. *Any question but that one.* "Because they think I'm dead," she announced baldly.

Jarek blinked. *Have I just been hit upside the head without knowing it?* He wondered vaguely. *Maybe I should be seeing stars right now because I know she didn't say what I think she said.*

"I think you'd better explain that," he demanded.

Mattie ducked her head. "That's another long story, Jay. Do we have to go through this now?" she groaned.

"Explain," he gritted out.

"Tykota was my brother's best friend on the island. He and Kel were the same age. I worshipped the ground my brother walked on despite our age difference. He spent time with me, made me laugh, taught me how to spear fish, swim, surf, catch crabs and even free dive," Mattie said, releasing a quick smile.

Jarek smiled too because he was glad she was finally talking about the happy times. He was beginning to wonder if all her memories had been bad.

"What's free dive?" he asked.

"Diving without gear. There are contests all over the world to see how deep a person can go without coming up for air. Tests your lungs for air capacity, which Kel considered to be a challenge. I could go pretty deep, but he and Ty were really good at it. Ty especially, which is probably why he became a SEAL. He was at our house so much, it was like having two brothers instead of one. When his grandparents died, he became a permanent part of our family. He became my brother for real. He and Kel were inseparable, I remember that much. And there was laughter, so much laughter in our house. No one stayed mad at one another for very long. We were all just…happy. Happy to be alive, to be with each other.

Then one day, Ty left. To college, I assumed. But Kel stayed home and did his surfing thing. He won a lot of trophies doing what he loved. He probably could've done it professionally, but then he met Melaina. Anyway, Ty would call a few times a week, and I remember talking to him when he did. And then the calls stopped coming altogether. My mother told me that he would be busy for a while and wouldn't be able to call as often. I understood that, I guess, but that didn't keep me from asking about him all the time. I hadn't seen him in such a long time, I was afraid I would forget what he looked like.

Melaina ended up pregnant with twins and I was too excited about becoming an aunt to badger my parents about Ty."

"What were the babies names?" Jarek asked.

"Neilani and Tabica, fraternal twins, and only three when..." Mattie trailed off and waved a hand in the air. "Well, you know."

Jarek felt a sharp stab of sympathy in the vicinity of his heart. His little sister, Kiri, was three years old and he spoiled her rotten. He didn't know what he would do, what his parents would do, if something ever happened to that little girl.

"What happened to Kel's wife? Was she..." he couldn't finish the thought.

"Oh, they weren't married. There had been some talk, but no date. She's still alive, as far as I know. But how alive can a mother be after losing her children and the man she loves, y'know? She wasn't there when it happened, but I bet she wishes she *had* been. There's not a day that goes by that I wonder why my life was spared," she said with a shrug.

"So why do your relatives think you're dead?" Jarek went back to the comment she'd made earlier.

"Ty enlisted in the Navy and became a SEAL. The phone calls stopped because he was always on assignment for months at a time. But something went wrong with one of his assignments. A leak, wrong info, I don't know for sure, " Mattie began to explain.

"Your family was murdered because of him, weren't they?" he asked bluntly.

"Jay—"

"People in his line of work make enemies, Mattie. I've gathered *that* much from watching spy movies."

"Tykota is *not* a spy, Jar—"

"Whomever he pissed off found his weakness. You and your family," his voice rose to drown out hers.

"Jarek—"

He sat up and turned to face her, his anger reaching the surface once again. "Tell me I'm wrong, Mattie. Tell me I'm wrong," he demanded.

"You're not wrong," she admitted without hesitation.

"How can you look at that man everyday knowing he took your family—"

"Shut up!" she shouted.

Judah jumped up on all fours, teeth bared, growling low in his throat. She caught him at his collar just as he was about to lunge at Jarek.

"Judah, sit," she commanded with a light jerk.

When he defied her, she repeated the command again and jerked harder. He sat on his haunches, statue still, pale blue eyes so much like Mattie's, boring holes into Jarek's person. He looked like he wanted to tear him apart. Jarek froze, his heart beating a wild tattoo. How was it that he seemed to forget this animal was in the room with them? And that he wasn't some overprotective Dobie, but an overprotective, semi-tame wolf? Jarek didn't look at Judah at all, just kept his gaze trained on Mattie's face and forced his limbs to loosen up.

Mattie pursed her lips and glared at him, too.

"If we're still going to continue to be partners in this contest, I'm going to have to explain something to you. You have *no right* to judge my situation when you don't know all the facts and you *sure* as hell don't know anything about Tykota," she pointed an accusing index finger at him.

Jarek nodded, instantly contrite. He'd overstepped his bounds. He wouldn't be surprised if she kicked him out, never to talk to him again. He wished he could take the words back, knowing he had broken the already fragile bond between them. He would have to bust his butt to get back to where they had been before he'd opened his big mouth.

"You're right. I don't know anything about him and I shouldn't have said what I did. I apologize," he said sincerely.

Mattie searched his face for a long moment. "Apology accepted," she said.

But he knew nothing would be the same. At least, not for a while. She was still wary, probably wondering why she had told him anything in the first place.

"So help me understand," he pleaded, hands out in supplication.

Mattie glanced at her watch, gave Judah a warning command, stood up, and started moving to the doorway.

"I think we've said enough already," she murmured softly.

Apparently that was his cue to leave, so he got up to follow her. His gaze ran over her, taking in the braid that no longer fell to her waist, but now rested between her shoulder blades

"Mattie."

Mattie paused and turned to him. Suddenly she felt so old. Old and tired.

"I don't want to argue anymore, Jarek. And I don't want you to be mad at me, either. It's going to be hard enough to concentrate on this contest after spilling my guts to you, and we can't afford any mess-ups on Friday. So how 'bout a truce?" she suggested, holding out her hand.

Jarek took it and used it as leverage to pull her into his arms. Instead of kissing her again, like he wanted to, he

CELISE DOWNS

wrapped her up tight and rocked from side to side. It was a hug she didn't realize she'd needed until his arms had twined around her shoulders.

"I'm sorry about the childhood you lost, Mattie," he whispered into her hair.

Mattie snuggled her head deeper into his chest. "Me, too."

With one last squeeze, she released him and stepped away. She gave him a small smile as he pulled his hair into a ponytail.

"Thanks for that," she said. "The hug, I mean."

Jarek smiled back. "My pleasure."

CHAPTER TEN

Thursday

"You cut your hair!" Ren shrieked when she saw Mattie the next morning at their lockers.

"I can't believe you cut your hair, *cherie*," Mici commiserated, reaching out to fluff the shoulder-length strands.

"Gawd, Mattie, your hair was your pride and joy," Ren continued to gush.

"It was so long. Almost to your butt, *oui*?" Mici questioned.

"It was time for a change," Mattie said.

"Gosh, well, it was quite a change," Ren claimed, running a hand down the back of Mattie's head. "Couldn't you have weaned us more slowly? Y'know, like an inch at a time or something?"

"Never mind her, *mon ami*. It suits you. What did Ty say?" Mici asked.

"He was the one who cut it," Mattie replied.

"It was his idea?" Ren asked in disbelief, eyes wide.

Mattie chuckled. "No. It was mine. It was just...time."

Mici stared at Mattie a moment before saying, "So, Jarek came over last night, *oui*?"

"Oui," Mattie parroted back, glancing over the books she needed to take with her.

"And?" Ren prodded.

"All went well. Ty approved, Judah didn't bite him. All went well," Mattie said, stuffing a Chemistry book and a spiral notebook in her backpack.

"That's it? Nothing else?" Mici asked casually, eyeing herself in the little mirror hanging on the inside of her locker.

"We practiced the routine," Mattie fibbed. It wasn't a total lie. The plan *had* been top practice, but well, plans can change.

"Nothing else?" she probed.

Mattie paused and turned her head. "What else, *exactly*, do you want to know?" she asked warily.

Mici stared back, saying nothing for a few seconds. "I do a reading on you guys every few months or so. I didn't know exactly when it would happen, but I saw a male. Someone other than Tykota," she explained.

Ren popped up next to them, her face in close proximity. "Did this Jarek dude make a pass at you?" she asked in a breathy whisper.

Mattie released a short giggle and rolled her eyes.

"If you mean did he throw me on the ground and ravish me, then no, he didn't make a pass at me. He just kissed me."

Ren's jaw dropped and Mici's expression became smug.

"He *kissed* you?"

"I knew it."

Mici and Ren spoke in unison, practically shoving her into her locker with excitement. Mattie laughed again and shook her head. She closed her locker, twisting the combination lock.

"When?"

"Where did it happen?"

"Did it curl your toes?"

"Is he a great kisser?"

"Which goes with the assessment that it would curl your toes."

"Did he use tongue?"

"That is so vulgar, Ren. You hang around those skaters too much. You're becoming unladylike. The word I think you're trying to say is French kiss."

Her friends lambasted her with questions, making Mattie laugh even harder. She'd been so busy, she'd forgotten to tell them. Or maybe she'd just wanted to keep it to herself for a while. She wasn't used to sharing personal moments with other people. It was something she would have to get used to.

"Would you two stop. You're acting like some miracle happened or something," she chided.

"A miracle *did* happen, *mon ami.* You're the first one out of all of us to have been kissed by a guy. A toe-curling, bone-tingling kind of kiss, I mean," Mici said.

"And the sloppy ones we got in the first grade don't count," Ren added.

"I find that very hard to believe," Mattie scoffed. "I've heard about your dates."

"Believe it," Ren quipped. "I'm a tomboy at heart, y'know? A guy would have to peel me off the vert ramp to kiss me, let alone talk to me. Which is why the only man for me is Tony Hawk," she said with a shrug, as if that were the only logical choice.

"And I think guys are a little turned off with the whole New Age thing. Too spooky or something," Mici added with a shrug.

And then there's me with my secret, Mattie thought. *Geez, we are really something. It's like we should be in counseling or rehab.*

"Well, to answer your questions, yes to everything. Although, the first kiss was—"

"The *first* kiss?" the girls chorused.

Mattie froze in place, not daring to look around. She hunched her shoulders and slipped her backpack on. There was a reason why she liked to keep her private life private and this was one of those reasons. No one, but *no one*, could have a private conversation in the locker area without everyone else knowing your business. For someone as closemouthed as Mattie, this was like having a bikini wax.

"So, he kissed you—"

Mattie held up one hand to stop Ren from saying anything more. "I'm done. That's it. He kissed me. Twice. And it was great. Both times. That's all I'm going to say so don't mention it again," she stated firmly.

"Fine. Let's talk about the investigation then. Has Ty found out anything yet?" Ren switched gears.

Mattie's mouth dropped open and she all but stumbled over her own feet trying to herd the girls out of the locker area and away from the crowds.

"Can you keep your voice down, please? We don't want to cause a school-wide panic," she hissed at Ren. "And I thought we agreed you wouldn't tell her?" she shot Mici an accusing glare.

"Well, why not? We're both up to our ears in the contest," Ren protested before Mici could respond.

"I didn't actually *say* I agreed with you, Mattie. I just nodded," Mici pointed out.

"Arrggh," Mattie growled out, slapping her hands on her legs.

"What was the big deal, anyway? How come you didn't want to tell me what was going on?" Ren demanded, hands on hips.

Mattie crossed her arms over her chest, shifted her weight to one leg, tilted her head, and quirked eyebrow.

"Did she try and talk you into dropping out of the contest?" she asked knowingly.

Ren bit her lip and glanced nervously at Mici, who had her head down. She shifted from foot to foot, making her wallet chain jingle.

"Yeah, she did," Ren finally admitted in a low voice.

"Uh-huh. And you wanted to know why I didn't want her to say anything to you," Mattie retorted wryly.

"I just wanted her to know, Mattie. She's part of the contest, too, and she had a right to know what was going on. She's your best friend, too, by the way. In case you've forgotten," Mici said quietly, pushing her glasses up with one finger.

"Okay, yeah, fine. But you should've known she wouldn't drop out. Both of us were lucky to have gotten this far. But Ty knows what he's doing. If he thought we were in danger, he would've said something to me," Mattie assured them.

"Well, that makes sense," Ren agreed. "He would never let anything happen to her."

Especially not after what happened ten years ago, Mattie thought.

"Did you make the bracelets?" Ren asked.

"Oh! Yeah, I did." Mici rummaged through her book bag until she found the pieces of jewelry made out of hematite beads.

She passed them out and Ren, who was all about wearing multiple bracelets anyway, eagerly put hers on. Mattie did the same.

"Well, I guess we'd better get a move on," Ren said, just as the warning bell rang.

"Yeah, I'll see you guys at lunch, okay?" Mattie returned, before turning away.

"Where are we goin' today?" Ren asked.

Mattie turned around, letting out a bark of laughter. "We've got two choices: Jack's or Guido's Deli."

"Actually, we have three now. They opened up a Bagel De Lox place that serves sandwiches as well as way tasty bagels," Mici interjected.

"I forgot about that. I can't wait 'til they start developing that dirt lot across the street from the school. Somebody's going to sooner or later," Mattie said.

"Yeah. They need to build somethin' over there so the students will stop getting arrested at those desert parties," Ren drawled.

"Are you done primping yet, Mic? We're going to be late," Mattie teased her friend, who had pulled out a hand mirror. "You look fine. You just left your house fifteen minutes ago, for crissakes."

Mici grumbled something in French and Mattie didn't bother to ask her to translate. Probably wouldn't have been worth repeating.

***

That day, Jarek found himself ditching his last class to drive to Mattie's house. He'd found it difficult to sleep last night, and concentrate today, after hearing her story. The sight of the jagged scars marring her beautiful skin kept rising up in his mind, making his hands and teeth clench. But they didn't matter to him. He still liked her, maybe was even a little in love with her. He was just glad she had survived her ordeal, and that Tykota had been there for her.

Jarek was still beating himself up over the things he'd said about the man. After his open-mouth-insert-foot disease had kicked in, he realized he was skating on thin ice with Mattie now. Apologizing to her hadn't been enough. It hadn't felt...right. He needed to apologize to Tykota, too. He didn't want to believe ill will of the man that had practically raised her from childhood, but Mattie hadn't said one word in his defense. Nor had she explained why her relatives thought she was dead. He needed answers and she had left him with no choice but to find them on his own.

As he pulled into the circular dirt driveway, Jarek found himself thinking what a cool looking house Mattie and Tykota lived in. He'd had some idea from last night that the house was pretty high-tech. Now that he was able to get a look in the daylight, he noticed it was the most unusual house in the area. All the other acres had that farm theme going on, and were nothing like this modernized stone and glass structure. As he got out of his car, Jarek glanced around, seeing things he hadn't seen last night. The landscaping was grassy with a few dozen palm trees. There was a silver Hum-V parked in front of the closed garage door with the words Black Hawk Protection Agency emblazoned on the side in red. And the lens of a surveillance camera, embedded in the stone near the top of the door, peered down at him as he rang the doorbell. Tykota opened the door seconds later.

"Hello, Jarek. Was Mattie expecting you today?" Tykota greeted. *And this early in the day?* Were the unspoken words that he didn't say.

"Um, no, actually. I came here to talk to you. Sir," Jarek said, removing his sunglasses.

Tykota nodded once and stepped back to allow him entry.

"I am on the phone right now, but please, make yourself comfortable in the family room," he said, pointing straight ahead as he headed down a hallway.

Jarek walked in and tucked his sunglasses down the front of his T-shirt.

"Do not worry about the wolves. They are out roaming," Tykota called over his shoulder.

"Thank God for that," Jarek mumbled, stepping around the wall and down into the sunken room.

Tykota had obviously seen the tentative steps he'd taken, not to mention the quick sweeping look he'd given his immediate surroundings. He didn't think he could get comfortable with two wolves staring at him like they wanted to rip his legs off. Although he'd met Judah, he hadn't met the other one and really wasn't in the mood to pass another test right now. The room had a cozy atmosphere with its overstuffed couch and sturdy oak furniture. The view out the sliding glass doors was something one didn't see too often in the desert: a sparkling pool surrounded by thigh-high blinding green grass rippling in the breeze. Actually, it could've been a mirage in the middle of the desert.

But what drew his attention was the collage of pictures on one wall. Taking a step closer, he noticed that they were all of Mattie at different stages in her life. They weren't black and white or color photos, but the brown tinted color that brought old-fashioned pictures to mind. Stepping back to get the full effect, he let his eyes drift over the wall of photographs and watched Mattie grow up. There was some of her when she was younger, probably when she had first come to live with Tykota. There was Mattie, standing in a field of flowers and wearing a wide-brimmed floppy hat; Mattie sitting on a rope swing, floral dress bunched around her thighs with strands of hair blowing in her face; Mattie reclining between the legs of a younger Tykota; Mattie sleeping in a hammock with Judah keeping watch nearby.

The next set was the preteen stage; Mattie standing on the rope swing and holding on with one hand, waist-length hair and the other hand flying out behind her. He'd never seen a smile so wide on her face before; Mattie leaning over the front porch railing to catch raindrops on her tongue; Mattie being lifted over the head of some man. And the pose where she was sitting on the rope swing, dress bunched around her thighs, strands of hair in her face showed up again. It was amazing how the photographer had caught her in that exact same pose years later.

She hadn't been smiling in the first picture and she wasn't smiling in this one, either.

The final set was the present with Mattie leaning against the Hum-V; Mattie dressed in a floral sarong and kneeling in front of a tree surrounded by white crosses; Mattie going through her routine at the barre in the studio; Mattie and two other girls running through the field of grass, wide smiles creasing their faces; Mattie standing amidst a group of men, arms crossed over her chest, legs apart, gazing unsmilingly into the lens.

These are Tykota's men, Jarek thought, taking a step closer to get a better look. In black T-shirts, black pants, black baseball hats with the initials ZSI stitched in silver, and combat boots, they looked like the government's version of American Gladiators. There were five men altogether and Jarek easily picked out Tykota. He also picked out the man that had lifted Mattie over his head in a previous picture. The two pictures that he particularly liked were the only two color photos out of the whole collection.

One was a close-up headshot of Mattie and the wolves. She was lying on her stomach with the wolves lying on either side of her. At that height, all three of their heads were at the same level, emphasizing the fact that they all possessed the same pale blue eyes. The background was pastel and had been photographed in a soft, ethereal glow, giving off an eerie but beautiful effect. Mattie had worn a heavy white turtleneck sweater, probably Tykota's, and had smoothed her hair up into an elegant bun on top of her head. She was wearing the barest hint of a smile and she seemed…content.

The one he favored, however, was an eight by ten that he wouldn't mind enlarging and hanging on his *own* wall. Mattie was wearing a floor-length ice blue gown and matching high-heeled sandals. Her make-up was model perfect and she'd let her thick mane of dark wavy hair cascade down her back. Standing in front of a snowy white background and sheer dove gray sheets blowing in a generated wind, the picture had been taken when Mattie had just finished spinning around. Arms flung out and hair flying in a perfect fan around her head, the camera had captured a smile so genuine he'd only seen it once: at the dance contest a few days ago.

"Ah. You have discovered my vice."

Jarek jumped at the sound of Tykota's voice. He glanced over his shoulder at him, then turned back to the wall of pictures.

"Mattie?"

"As well as photography," Tykota replied, hands behind his back.

Jarek looked back at him in surprise. "You took all of these?"

"Yes. I try to take as many as possible. Children grow up quick," Tykota commented.

"Don't I know it," Jarek commiserated.

Tykota stared at Jarek with narrowed eyes. "You have children?"

Jarek's jaw dropped open and he felt his eyes bulge out of his head.

"Are you *crazy*? I'm too young to have kids. I mean, I love kids and want to have some. Eventually. I was talking about my little sister, Kiri. She's three and every day she has a new word or facial expression," he explained.

"Mm. Then you *do* know what I mean," Tykota waved a hand towards the couch. "Please. Have a seat. Would you like something to drink?" he offered.

Jarek moved to the couch, sat down, and crossed an ankle over the opposite knee. "Thanks, but no."

"Then what can I do for you?" Tykota inquired, taking a chair at an angle with the couch.

Jarek forced himself to look at the man directly, even though his heart tried to beat itself out of his chest. He'd never done this before. But he didn't have anything to hide so there was no reason for him *not* to look the man in the face.

"I don't know if Mattie told you anything about yesterday..." he began, raising an eyebrow in question.

"I have a feeling she talked about her childhood," was all he said.

"She did. She told me everything and I...said something I shouldn't have and I'd like to apologize," the words came out rushed despite his earlier reassurance that he wasn't nervous.

"Like I said, Mattie is not home—"

"I'm apologizing to *you,* Mr. Black Hawk. Sir," Jarek interrupted.

Tykota's head jerked back in surprise, onyx eyes searching Jarek's face.

"Tykota."

Jarek blinked in confusion. "Excuse me?"

"Tykota," he repeated. "My name is Tykota. Or Ty, if you prefer."

Jarek nodded slowly. "O-okay. Ty."

"You are apologizing to me? I do not understand."

Jarek cleared his throat and moved his gaze to the view of the backyard.

"I—Mattie told me what you do for a living. Then and now," he paused and returned his attention back to Tykota.

Tykota steepled his fingers together and braced them against his mouth. "I see."

"I had assumed Mattie's family had been murdered because of you," Jarek blurted without preamble.

Tykota's head came up sharply and his face tightened. When he said nothing, Jarek continued.

"She didn't deny it. What I don't understand, and what she won't tell me, is why her relatives think she's dead."

Tykota inhaled deeply and released it in a low sigh. He levered himself out of the chair and turned to look out the sliding glass doors. Jarek's body relaxed after he'd self-consciously tensed up with the man's movement.

"I *am* her relative," Tykota stated in a quiet voice.

"But not by blood. Mattie said her parents adopted you," Jarek relayed.

"Yes, that is true."

When nothing else was forthcoming, Jarek realized the man wasn't going to make this easy for him. Well, that was fine with him. He liked challenges and being a part of Mattie's life was definitely going to be a challenge.

"Her relatives think she's dead. I want to know why," he repeated his earlier statement.

Tykota settled his hands on his hips.

"When she was taken to the hospital that day, she was half dead. She had lost a lot of blood before the paramedics had arrived. You saw her injuries, I imagine," he glanced over his shoulder.

Jarek nodded in confirmation.

"I was there for a half hour, watching them try to save her, when they pronounced her dead. I told her relatives the news and convinced them they didn't want to see her body. She was bloody and cut up, her clothes had been torn, her eyes..." he shook his head at the memory. "No one should see their kin like that, especially a child. That is not the last memory I wanted them to have of Mattie. A nurse was in the room, putting equipment away, when she heard a beep. They could not believe it. *I* could not believe it. She was alive."

Jarek was transfixed. Seems both Mattie and Tykota had interesting stories to tell

"I was a Navy SEAL. Did she tell you that?" Tykota glanced over his shoulder again.

"Yes," Jarek answered.

"During one of those assignments, my Extraction Unit was...compromised. I cannot tell you the logistics of the assignment because, as you know, everything is Top Secret. But we did exactly what the name of our unit states. We dealt with mostly hostage situations and we did whatever necessary to bring the hostage home. But we were betrayed. Our identities were revealed. I did not find out the repercussions of that assignment until I reached stateside. By then it was too late. Mattie was the only one who had survived because someone had come along.

While she was trying to recover, there was another attempt on her life. No one knew she was still alive except for the hospital staff and me. Was there a leak?" he shrugged.

"I doubt it. They were probably just doing their job. I just had not done mine too well. The sonuvabitch had tried to take her out again. On *my* watch. I was not about to let that happen again, so I took her off the island and brought her to the reservation where I was born. I felt she would be safer there. Not long after that, I discharged out of the military and started working for Zion Security," Tykota concluded.

He moved back to the armchair and smoothly dropped into it, his black eyes probing Jarek's face. Jarek had turned his head to study the wall of photographs again, his eyes snagging on the one where Mattie was holding the bushel of flowers under her nose.

"Do you understand now?" Tykota asked in a low tone.

Jarek glanced down at his lap, then back up at the wall of pictures. This time, his eyes found his favorite photo.

"I understand."

"Do you have any more questions?"

With one last glance at the picture, he turned his gaze back to Tykota. "Yeah. Whatever happened to the person who betrayed you?"

"Dead."

"And the person who murdered Mattie's family?"

"He's dead."

At the unexpected female voice, Jarek hopped up off the couch with a guilty start and whirled around.

"Mattie," he said in surprise.

"What the hell are you doing here?"

CHAPTER ELEVEN

Thursday

"**M**attie," Tykota warned in a low tone.

"I came to get some answers," Jarek said, stuffing the tips of his fingers in his front pockets.

Mattie let out a huff. "I was going to tell you, Jay."

"When?"

"After the contest tomorrow," she told him.

"I couldn't wait that long," Jarek claimed.

Mattie sighed and shifted her weight to one leg. "I can't believe you came here."

"What did you expect me to do, Mattie? You refused to tell me anything. How could you expect me to go on working with you knowing how I felt about him? You could've defended him at anytime, but you didn't. You might be able to hide your feelings and pretend that everything's all right when it's really not, but I can't. That's not the way I am."

Jarek paused, glanced at Tykota, then back at Mattie. "Besides, I owed him an apology."

Mattie turned an icy glare on Tykota.

"You sent him to the studio yesterday, didn't you?" she accused in his native language. "You knew I wasn't ready for company yet."

"It is time for you to let someone else in, Mattie. Someone besides Renee and Michelle," he responded in kind. "This boy cares about you a lot. Probably even loves you. He was mighty brave to confront me on his own without interference from you. I think that is admirable," he added, one eyebrow raised.

Just as quickly as it flared, Mattie's anger deflated and she looked back at Jarek. He hadn't taken his eyes off of her since she'd entered the room. She sighed and looked down at the floor. She ran a hand over her hair, flicking her braid over her shoulder. She still had to get used to the shorter style, but it was growing on her.

"Where are the wolves?" she asked in English.

"Out playing," Tykota answered, jerking his head towards the sliding glass doors. "They will be coming in for a snack soon."

Mattie raised her head to look at Jarek. "You'll have to be introduced to Dar," she said.

Jarek shrugged a shoulder. "Fine. Whatever."

"Did you ..come over for anything else?" she asked tentatively.

"Well, talking to Tykota was my main gig, but I thought we could go over the routine one last time. Y'know, since we didn't get around to it yesterday. I don't wanna tire you out or anything, but maybe we could run through it a couple of times," he said, letting his gaze drift over her.

"Okay. Well. Let me put my stuff down. You remember how to get to the studio?" Mattie asked.

Jarek nodded. "Yeah."

He turned to Tykota and held out his right hand. "Thanks, Ty."

"You are very welcome, Jarek," he replied with a half smile, shaking the proffered hand.

Mattie watched Jarek stride down the hall in the opposite direction, then turned to go to her room.

"Mataya." Tykota's voice stopped her before she took one step, but she didn't look at him. She waited, saying nothing.

"You will have to tell him about the assignment."

Mattie nodded. "I know. I'll tell him now," she said, then turned away.

"Mattie", Ty called to her.

Mattie paused to look back at him. When he stepped around the couch and came towards her, she turned to face him.

"Despite what anyone else says, or thinks, I do not regret lying to your relatives. I love you, Mataya. I always will and that will never change. I only wanted to keep you safe. It was the only way," he said, pulling her into a hug and burying his chin in her hair.

" I know. I didn't hate you for it then and I don't hate you for it now. I didn't tell Jarek anything because *I* knew why you did what you did and I thought that's all that mattered," she explained.

Tykota leaned back, his arms still around her shoulders.

"Jarek wants to be a part of your life, sweetling. You cannot hold him off with half-truths and lies. He is not like Renee and Michelle. Jarek is persistent, as you obviously noticed, and he is not going to go away quietly when you want to avoid talking about certain things," he pointed out.

Mattie sighed again and bowed her head until her forehead touched his chest.

"I know. It's just that, for so long...I guess I'm used to being cautious, to thinking very carefully before speaking. And secrecy was such a big part of what you used to do, I guess it just rubbed off or something," she shrugged.

Tykota released her and ran both hands over her head.

"So you re-evaluate your life to include Renee and Michelle...and Jarek. You have friends now, sweetling. Friends who share pieces of their lives with you and who expect you to do the same in return. You cannot keep pushing people away. You will only end up alone. I know you love me, and the other guys, as well. The feeling is deeply mutual," he said.

"But?" Mattie urged with a raised eyebrow.

"But you need something else, *someone* else, in your life. I am not always going to be here," he paused to hold up a finger when she opened her mouth to protest. "I am not talking about losing my life on the job. I am talking about natural causes. If I had an accident, you will need someone to be there with you."

Mattie leaned back in his arms and looked up at him, head tilted to one side.

"But what if it's *not* an accident?"

Tykota sighed and shook her gently. "Do not twist my words into something ugly, my love. Do you understand what I am trying to say?" he chided.

"I understand, but do you blame me for thinking that way? Look what happened to Kedren and his friends. And me and my family," she pointed out.

"Yes, but you cannot dwell on the bad when something good has come out of it. Kedren and his friends found the man they were looking for. Kedren and Skylar fell in love and will be getting married, did you forget? And look at you now, Mattie. We found the man who took your family away. We found the man who hurt you and made sure he would not be able to hurt anyone ever again. And you have *me* now. You have me and four other men who will always love you, protect you, and look out for you. But you also have Renee and Michelle...and Jarek. There is good in your life now, Mattie. Do not throw it away." Tykota smoothed his hands over her head again before framing her face. He placed a kiss on her forehead then walked away.

"I will be bringing the boys in after a while," he threw over his shoulder.

She didn't know if that required a comment or not, so she decided not to make one. She went back to her room and brushed out her hair, thinking that everything was moving too fast. She should've known on some level that Jarek wouldn't leave it alone. Mattie had a feeling his persistent nature was genetic. Liz could be just as stubborn sometimes.

As for the possible situation with DJP, well, Jarek probably should've been the first person to know. Liz was his aunt, his *only* aunt, and he never would've forgiven her if something had happened to her when she could've done something to stop it. Would he be mad anyway? Something was supposed to go down within the next couple of days. Would he get angry if she were just now telling him?

"Well, you're about to find out," she murmured to her image in the mirror.

She found him standing at the glass wall, taking in the view of the backyard, legs spread, arms crossed over his chest. He wasn't aware of her presence yet so she took a moment to openly gaze upon him. She wouldn't have been able to tell a soul what he'd been wearing when she'd first arrived. She hadn't been in the best of moods to find him here in the first place.

His jet-black hair had been slicked back into a ponytail, emphasizing his chiseled profile. And boy, did he have a great profile. Her eyes moved down to the rather unique tank top he was wearing. It was white, but suspender-like straps were holding up the ribbed material instead of the usual cloth straps. Mattie had never seen one like it before and found she wanted one for herself. Faded Levi's hung low on his hips and scuffed hiking boots completed an outfit that made him look down right gorgeous. *Would he be able to dance in those?* She wondered.

When she stepped into the studio, Jarek turned around and leaned against the wall, arms still crossed over his chest. His gaze swept over her from head to toe, before settling on her face. The half smile on his face let her know that he liked what he saw, maybe even remembered the outfit. She wondered what his reaction would be to her actual costume.

"You cut your hair," he announced into the silence.

Mattie grinned and ran a self-conscious hand through the strands.

"Yeah. Thought it was time for a change," she said.

Jarek nodded and began to lazily stride towards her, shoving his hands in his back pockets. *How could he make something so mundane as putting his hands in his pockets look so sexy?* She wondered.

"I like it. It looks good," he said, his eyes never leaving her face.

She stepped farther into the room, clasping her hands behind her back. She was nervous. And she had a feeling it was the way Jarek was stalking her, his green eyes ever watchful. He jerked his head towards the glass wall, but he never once broke his stride. Or his gaze.

"It really is beautiful here where you guys live. I never thought a place like this could exist in Arizona," he said.

"What—you've never seen green fields and palm trees? There are tons of those around here," she retorted, standing with her weight on one leg while she swung the other in a wide arc.

Jarek rolled his eyes as a crooked grin kicked up one corner of his mouth.

"Yeah. Who hasn't," he replied in amusement, glancing over his shoulder. "But this is different. This is something you'd find…" he trailed off, trying to think of a place where he *would* find it.

"On an island," Mattie supplied softly, her own eyes moving to the view beyond him.

"Yeah. On an island." He paused, noticing the wistful expression on her face.

"Does this place remind you of home?" he asked quietly.

"This *is* my home," she corrected him.

"I meant your birth home. Hawaii," he clarified.

"Yes." Her response was quick and her eyes flickered.

"Did Ty move you here because it reminded you of your home?" Jarek asked, stepping closer.

Mattie blinked in rapid succession as though she was trying to keep tears at bay. "That, too. I'm sure he told you some stuff," she said, pale blue eyes focusing on him.

"Umm, he told me why he brought you to Zion Headquarters. He didn't say why he brought you *here*," Jarek said.

"I was homesick. My recovery wasn't...progressing. The environment wasn't exactly the right place for a trauma victim to heal. It was too stark, too...clinical, I guess. The building itself is all black, chrome and glass. The furniture in my room was like...futuristic modern. It wasn't homey. It wasn't comfortable. There was a feeling of...it was a utility room. A place where the field operatives could come for a little R and R, but not to live, y'know? So Ty and his men did some scouting around and found this land. Zion cleared it and built the house to Ty's specs," she explained with a winsome smile.

"So he designed the place, huh? And Zion built it?" he asked in disbelief.

"Yep."

"Wow. It's great. I mean, it's a really cool place," he praised, scanning the studio. "With all the amenities of a Sci-Fi movie," he added jokingly.

Mattie released a chuckle. "Yeah. It took me a while to get used to some of this stuff, but as time went by, it began to grow on—" she broke off abruptly as she flicked a glance at his chest. And did a doubletake.

"Jarek, you have a tattoo." Mattie said the words in the same tone as "You have a hickey on your neck."

Jarek laughed at the one-eighty degree turn in conversation. The tank top he wore didn't quite hide the piece of art permanently stamped on his right pec. He forgot that not everyone knew about the tattoo. He pretty much forgot himself since it was covered up the majority of the time.

"I know I do," he said in response to her revelation.

"But...I never knew you had a tattoo," she said with a laugh. "Do your parents know?"

"Yeah. They weren't too happy about it at first, though."

"What's it of? Can I see?" she asked, taking a step closer to him.

"Sure." Jarek pulled the suspender down and watched as her smile grew wider.

It was a baby pin with the words KIRI written in cursive on the top half, while a diaper dangled from the bottom half. Mattie laughed again and without thinking, ran a fingertip over it. Jarek's skin broke out with goosebumps and his pec muscle jumped with the contact. As if suddenly realizing how close she was, and that she'd touched him, Mattie released a nervous smile and stepped away.

"Who's Kiri?" she asked.

"My little sister. She's three," Jarek answered.

Mattie's smile dimmed and he was once again reminded of all she had told him about her past. A past that had, at one time, included three-year-old fraternal twins.

"She's that special, huh?" Mattie asked in a soft voice.

"Yeah," he murmured, pulling the strap back up. "She's a miracle baby, really. My Mom was told that she couldn't have any more children after me. And then along came Kiri. There were complications, of course. During and after, but we all wanted this so bad that we fought for her. They even let me name her," he explained with a smile.

Mattie's eyes widened in delight. "They did? How'd you come up with the name?"

Jarek's expression became sheepish and if she wasn't mistaken, he actually...blushed? Yes, he blushed.

"It was going to be the name of my *own* daughter, actually. Some day," he admitted.

Mattie couldn't have been more surprised if she'd been slapped upside the head with a wet leotard. She crossed her legs and sank gracefully to the floor. Jarek followed suit, taking a position opposite her.

"So you want children." It wasn't a question.

"Eventually, yeah. Taking care of Kiri gives me practice. But I love it, though. I love *her*. I mean, I love playing with her, giving her baths, taking her out to the park or to the store. She's such a happy and well-behaved baby, y'know? Every day she learns something new, does some new trick, a new facial expression. I'd always wanted a brother or sister, but was told it could never happen. When my Dad and I found out Mom was pregnant, we cried." Jarek shook his head at the memory. "I've never seen my Dad cry before. Well, he wasn't actually crying, it was more like bawling his head off," he amended.

Mattie laughed.

"When they saw how gung-ho I was about the whole thing, they let me choose the name. And they liked it."

"Kiri what? Did you give her a middle name?"

"It's pronounced Dayanera, but I spelled it D-e-i-a-n-e-i-r-a, " he told her.

"Kiri Deianeira Thanos," she tested the name. "Sounds very Greek. I like it. It's a beautiful name."

Jarek smiled warmly as his eyes caressed her face.

"I'm glad you think so," he murmured, voice husky.

Mattie cleared her throat when she noticed his gaze move down to her mouth. "Jarek Logan has a pretty nice ring to it, too," she commented inanely.

"I'm glad you think so," he repeated. If it was possible, his voice became even huskier.

Mattie cleared her throat again and she refrained from licking her lips in a nervous gesture. Barely.

"I-I...my mother never gave Kel and me middle names, so when Ty adopted me, he gave me one," she stammered.

Momentarily distracted from what he'd been about to do, Jarek paused.

"Really? What name did he give you?" he inquired.

"Shadae. His first assignment as a field op for Zion was a kidnapping. The little girl he'd saved had reminded him of me because we had been the same age. Seven, that is. They formed such a great bond, he still sends her birthday cards to this day," Mattie explained.

"Mataya Shadae Black Hawk. It's a beautiful name," he said.

"I'm glad you think so," she repeated his own words with a teasing smile.

Jarek leaned in close to kiss her, and as much as she wanted him to, she couldn't let him. Not yet. She needed to tell him something first. Jerking her head back a fraction, Mattie placed two fingers over his mouth.

"I, uh, we need to talk. About something," she sputtered again, then swallowed audibly.

Jarek stared at her for a long moment before kissing her fingertips, then held her hand in both of his.

"Okay. What about?"

"Do you like coffee or tea? There's a Daily Grind down the street."

Jarek looked at her in disbelief. "Are you serious?"

"Very."

"What do you have to tell me that you can't tell me now? Are you afraid I'm going to do something?" he asked.

"Jay, you're going to have questions that might take time to answer," Mattie began to explain.

"What the hell is going on?" he asked in a low tone.

"And we know the routine by heart," she continued as though he hadn't said a word. "Just the other day, you said you could perform it in your sleep. To be honest, so can I, so there's no need to go over it again. So, is the Daily Grind okay? Or did you want to grab something to eat?"

Jarek didn't think he'd be able to handle anything more than liquid right now. At least, not until he found out what was going on.

"Daily Grind is fine," he said.

"Good. Let's go."

***

A half hour later, Jarek sat in stunned silence. It was a good thing he was already sitting down because he would've slid to the floor if she'd told the story while he'd been standing.

"Is there anything...*else* I should know?" he asked in a voice laden with delayed shock.

Mattie took a sip of her tea. "Well, um, not that I know of. Ty hasn't told me much more than that."

Good, because he didn't think he could take any more. Between Mattie's past and the current situation, he was beginning to wonder if he was going to have to reserve a rubber room and a straitjacket. He sighed and ran both hands over his head before tightening his ponytail with a quick jerk. He took a fortifying sip of his mocha latte.

"So, Liz isn't in any danger." It wasn't a question, but a clarification of what she'd just told him.

"No. All the victims have been *our* age."

"And they're all connected because they went to the same party?"

"No, not the same party. The same *evidence*," Mattie corrected. "A VIP Pass."

"Like a-a calling card or something?" Jarek asked.

Mattie tilted her head to the side. "I hadn't thought of it like that, but yeah, like a calling card."

Jarek leaned in close, wrapping his hands around his cup. "Sounds like something a serial killer would do. Ty thinks there's a connection to the show?"

"He didn't come right out and say that. It was more like an assumption. I mean, all the victims had the VIP Pass. That's pretty, y'know, odd, don't you think?"

Jarek sighed. "Yeah, okay, I guess. So, it's just kidneys? Nothing major?"

"Like what? Hearts and lungs? No. It seems like they're only taking stuff you can live without," Mattie expounded.

"And that includes…?"

"Besides kidneys? The spleen, maybe part of a liver, an eyeball, the gall bladder, reproductive organs," Mattie listed on her fingers. "But it's just been kidneys so far. None of that other stuff. Yet."

"So what would somebody want with a kidney?" Jarek asked.

Mattie sat back and just stared at him with wide eyes. Was it just her or did he live under a rock?

"What? What did I say?" he asked when she remained silent.

"Do you know what you just asked?"

Jarek glanced away then back at her. "Uh, yeah."

"Well, on the off chance that Hannibal Lecter isn't coming off a starvation diet, why *would* anyone want a kidney?" she retorted sarcastically, arms over her chest.

Let him chew on that *for a minute*, she thought with a slurp of tea. A minute later, when she saw the proverbial Light of Knowledge flicker across his face, Mattie smiled.

"Why not just get on a donor list?" he wanted to know.

"Because not everyone lives in America, Jay. Even then, do you know how long those lists are? *Long.* And you could be on one for years, Jay. *Years.* And there are no guarantees. Sometimes you get lucky. But most of the time, people aren't so lucky and they have to do whatever it takes."

"And Ty's involved because of his Agency?"

"He guards children. It's his job, what he does," Mattie said.

"So is that what *you* want to do?" he asked, thinking of the group shot hanging on the wall at her house.

Mattie glanced down at the table before taking a sip of her tea.

"If I want it, yes. I know he started the Agency because of me. It'll be mine eventually. But it'll be Plan C if Plan A or Plan B doesn't work out," she admitted truthfully.

Jarek took one of her hands in both of his and began to massage it. He looked up to gaze at her after concentrating on the movements of his fingers.

"So what's Plan A?" The huskiness had returned to his voice again.

"Plan A is Groovy Now Dance Studio. I'm planning on majoring in business in college and I'd like to open up a place like Rhythm Station," she revealed. "I love to dance and I don't think that will ever go away."

Jarek smiled. "Groovy Now Dance Studio. I like that," he said with a nod. "And Plan B?"

"Maikainai Island. Maikainai was the last name I was born with before it had to be changed," she divulged.

Jarek sensed that Maikainai Island was more important than the dance studio, so he stopped massaging her hand to listen to her answer when he asked, "And what is Maikainai Island?"

"It's a place where people will be able to go to heal. Y'know, people like me who have physical scars. I've been lucky to have Ty in my life, but I think I could've handled my feelings about the scars a lot better of I'd had someone else to talk to. Someone who had experienced what *I* had experienced, and had the scars to prove it. I was doing the therapy thing and the group sessions, but it was for dealing with the loss of my family. Losing my family wasn't the only thing I needed to deal with at the time, though.

If there had been a place like that, a place away from the stereotypical "clinical setting" of therapy, I probably wouldn't have kept my scars a secret for so long. Maikainai Island would be near my birth home, a place to go and heal, interact with patients, talk with professionals who've "been there". But it'll be a place where they get lessons in surfing, scuba diving, swimming, snorkeling, spear fishing, and hula dancing. Or they can just veg on the beach and go swimming.

It'll be a fun place where you can build up enough confidence to integrate yourself back into society without too many hang-ups about your physical scars," she concluded, taking a much needed breath of air. *Geez, where had* that *come from*? She asked herself in amazement.

Jarek sat and stared at her in stunned silence, his jaw dangling somewhere near the floor beside his chair. Neither one of them spoke for a long moment, until Jarek was finally able to break out of his shocked stupor.

***

Later on that afternoon, a beeper went off in the parking lot of a department store. A young man dug through his duffel bag to turn off the offending sound. He bit off a curse at the familiar set of numbers, then pulled out his cell phone. He really didn't need this right now.

"We need some more donors, Sonny," came the disembodied voice on the other end of the line.

"Getting more than one might be too risky this time," the young man said, glancing around the parking lot.

"Throw a party for the losers of that contest tomorrow," the voice demanded.

The young man's eyes nearly bugged at how many "losers" that would be.

"No way," he gritted out.

"There'll be big bucks for ya, Sonny. There always is," the voice coaxed.

"No. Way. Twelve is too many. And stop calling me Sonny."

"Don't disappoint, *Sonny.* You're in this up to your neck," the voice was angry now.

"Fine. But this is the last time," the young man rapped out, then flipped the cover down.

The last time, he vowed.

CHAPTER TWELVE

Friday/Showtime

"**H**ey everybody, welcome to a special two hour edition of *Dance Jam Productions*. We're your hosts, Pepe Carrington—"

"—And Downtown Sophie Brown. For those of you who've been living under a rock this week, we've been counting down to the Dance-Off tomorrow night."

"Twelve couples will compete, but only six will make it to the Bonus Round," Pepe said in his best game show host voice.

"Out of those six semi-finalists, only three couples will become new additions to our DJP team—"

"—But don't think we're gonna have any sore losers here. Oh no, no, no. For participating, our three runners up couples will receive a special VIP Pass to come on down and bust a move on *Dance Jam Productions* whenever they feel like it. Plus, there will be an after-party held for all twelve finalists at a special location, hosted by none other than Yours Truly," Pepe announced with a cheeky grin.

"And don't forget Yours Truliest," Sophie said with a grudging poke to Pepe's ribcage. "The DJP dancers will be making an appearance, too, so that should be a really fun time tomorrow night."

"*No* doubt," Pepe interjected.

"So, let's get this party started with our first contestants. Jamie Satterfield and Gabe Westin are both juniors at Devil Mountain High School and they're going to be dancing to Metallica's "Disappear" from the *Mission Impossible Two* soundtrack..."

Mattie, in the process of putting on her make-up on the female side of the dressing room, paused in the act of smoothing on lipstick to listen to the hosts. Ren, who was sitting beside her, squealed in excitement.

"I'm going to meet Chris. I'm going to meet Chris," she chanted as she bounced in her chair.

"You've already met Chris, Rennie," Mattie reminded her.

"Yeah, but that was only for a minute. This time, I'll actually be able to have a real conversation with him," she said with a cheek-cracking smile.

"Oh brother," Mattie murmured under her breath.

"I can't believe it. I really can't believe it," Ren went on.

"I'm overwhelmed," Mattie retorted drolly, then pressed her lips together to blend the lipstick.

"Aren't you excited, Mattie?" Ren bubbled.

"Totally…stoked. Can't you tell?" Mattie drawled, barely restraining an eye roll.

Ren huffed and tossed down her eye pencil.

"You could at least show some enthusiasm for getting this far, Mattie. We beat out hundreds of couples to get here. Doesn't that mean anything to you? Doesn't that make you feel like you've accomplished somethin'?"

Mattie glanced at her friend in the mirror, sighed, then placed her lipstick back in her make-up bag. Ren was right, of course. She was ruining this whole thing for her best friend, not to mention herself. *If only Ty's assignment had been anywhere else*, she thought wearily.

"I'm sorry, Ren. I'm glad we got this far. It's a great accomplishment for both of us…" she paused.

"But?" she urged.

"I'm just a little preoccupied, I guess. It's nothing," Mattie brushed away the thought with a wave of her hand.

Ren nudged her in the arm with her elbow. "Oh, c'mon. Don't hold out on me now. What's going on? It can't be the routine. You told me that you and Jarek could dance blindfolded."

Mattie shrugged. "No, it's not that. I'm just a little on edge with Ty's assignment. It's like I'm too worried to enjoy myself."

Ren's shoulders drooped. "I'd almost forgotten about that," she said softly.

"I wish I could forget, too, but unfortunately, I can't," Mattie admitted grudgingly.

"Do you think something will happen today?" Ren asked with a slight frown.

"No. Not today. But that party tomorrow night would be a prime opportunity," Mattie confessed, pulling out a tube of black mascara.

Ren blinked. "Sooooo...what are you saying?"

Mattie leaned towards the mirror and applied a few strokes to her lashes before answering.

"I'm just saying we're gonna be like Siamese twins joined at the hip. We go everywhere together."

"O-kay, now look. I love you an' all. You're my best friend, but I don't want people thinkin' that we're, y'know, *together*," Ren said, her Southern accent slipping out.

Mattie released a short bark of laughter, smearing her eyeliner across her eyelid.

"Dammit, Rennie," she cursed around a laugh. "You almost made me poke myself in the eye."

"Not my bad. It's your own fault for mentioning the Siamese twin thing," Ren replied breezily.

"I meant we just stick together, ya big dork. We go to the ladies room together, and if we're thirsty, the drinks are going to have to be in an unopened can or bottle. Nothing in a cup unless it's a cup of ice," Mattie explained.

Mattie swiped her left eyelid with a tissue and started over again, listening with half an ear to the constant chatter of the other girls. As she pulled her hair over one shoulder to brush it, she began to examine her surroundings.

The dressing room had been set up towards the back of the station and reminded Mattie of the dressing rooms in the auditorium at school. Waist-high counters and mirrors framed by bare, hot lightbulbs ran the length of both walls. Full-length mirrors could be found in the adjoining bathroom. Every so often, a female tech person with headphones and a clipboard in hand would come in and call out a couple of names. Little by little, their group dwindled, but would soon be replaced with a flushed contestant who had just performed. Excitement, anxiety, nerves. Mattie sensed it all and yet wasn't feeling any of it herself. She was, and always had been, amazingly calm under pressure. *That would be Ty's influence,* she thought with an inward smile.

"...For couple number seven. Jolie Fairchild is a sophomore at Lakeside High and Jackson Tolliver is a senior at Chaminade..."

Mattie snickered at the odd pairing. At Catalina Valley, the school she attended, sophomores and seniors didn't associate with one another. Unless they were forced to, that is. It was considered to be socially unacceptable and encouraged much razzing amongst the upperclassmen. Mattie didn't care one way or the other. She wasn't interested in any of the guys at her school anyway. And if any of them were interested in her, she wouldn't know or didn't care to find out.

"...Bustin' a move to Stabbing Westward's "Save Yourself" from *Tekken: The Movie,* lets give it up for couple number eight," Sophie was announcing enthusiastically.

"That's a pretty cool song," Mattie murmured.

"I'd have to agree with you on that," Ren added.

Mattie blinked in surprise, thinking no one had heard her. "It's one of those I-feel-like-hitting-something-stress-reliever type of songs," she went on, throwing her hair back over her shoulder.

"Definitely works for me," Ren retorted. "That's a really gorgeous outfit, Mattie," she added.

Mattie studied what she could of her reflection in the mirror. Smoothing both hands down the front of the lace outfit, she released a pleased grin.

"Thanks. You don't look so bad yourself," she reciprocated.

Ren was someone who took dancing seriously, so every time she went clubbing, she dressed to impress. Today was no different. Well, it was different to a certain point. Her burnished gold hair had been teased and hair-sprayed into a sassy style, and was contained by a cute white daisy barrette. Her green eyes had been dramatically enhanced with fake eyelashes and smoky eyeshadow, and blood red lipstick made a wicked slash across her mouth. However, it was her outfit that Mattie particularly envied. To her, it looked like Ren was wearing her underwear: a black bra with matching panties that were high cut on the sides. Over that, she wore a long-sleeved, bell bottomed, black mesh body suit with black and white polka dots on it; ruffles adorned her wrists and ankles. The black jazz shoes didn't do much for the outfit, but then again, there was the breaking-ones-leg-on-national-television factor to consider.

The fact that the bodysuit was as see through as cellophane would have a Bug-Out Eye Factor of about fifty quadrillion. If Ty had seen Mattie in that outfit, he would've locked her in her room until she was thirty. She would give her very life to be able to wear something as revealing as Ren's outfit, but there was one little problem: her body wasn't as perfect as Ren's.

Mattie released a sigh and absently wondered if they were really going to let her go on camera dressed like that. If anything, the ratings would go up. Like herself, Ren had chosen not to show her outfit to her partner. She'd wanted to go for shock value, which she had definitely achieved. What did Jamie look like in his Austin Powers velvet ensemble? Tonight was sure going to be interesting. *I wonder if Jarek's nervous.*

***

I wonder if Mattie's nervous, Jarek thought as he studied himself in the floor length mirror. She's probably preoccupied with Tykota's current assignment. He kept thinking that he should be cautious, too, but Tykota hadn't tried to stop her from being in the contest. That had to mean something, right? If Tykota thought she'd be in danger, he would've said something long before now.

As he tightened the bow tie, he studied himself critically. The tux had been an ingenious idea. A tuxedo was as a part of James Bond as all the hi-tech gadgets he used. Earlier this morning, he had tried the routine with the jacket on, but it hadn't worked. It had been too confining for the movements they'd choreographed. The original plan was for her to remove his jacket before the routine started and he decided to stick with that.

Jarek passed a hand over the jet-black hair he had slicked back into a ponytail. One side of his mouth kicked up at the reaction that would garner from Mattie. She had told him on more than one occasion that she didn't like his hair in a ponytail. He found that she liked it when it was down or in a partial ponytail. He did the latter more often than not, but James Bond personified debonair. A ponytail was about as debonair as he could get without cutting it all off.

His best friend, Gunner Simons, sidled up to him, threw an arm around his shoulder, and looked him up and down in the mirror.

"Pretty snazzy, J.T. Trying to the impress the ladies?" he teased.

Jarek smiled and tugged on his cuffs. "Only one lady in particular," he replied.

Gunner turned around and leaned against the wall so he could look at Jarek from the front.

"You really like this girl, don't you?" he asked, seriously.

"Yeah, I do," Jarek admitted truthfully. "She's different. I mean, we have the dance thing in common, but she's had so much to deal with that it's made her a stronger person."

Gunner crossed his arms over his chest. "Y'know, we haven't talked to each other in almost a week, man," he pointed out.

"Yeah, I know. This contest thing has pretty much taken up all my time," Jarek said, walking back into the main room to sit down on a chair.

"I imagine your partner took up more of your time than anything else," Gunner remarked with a knowing grin. "What's her name?"

"Mataya Black Hawk. But she prefers Mattie," Jarek answered, liking the way her name sounded on his tongue.

"So, what were you talking about a few minutes ago? Y'know, about her dealing with so much?" Gunner inquired, taking a chair across from Jarek.

"When she was seven, her whole family was murdered and she was the one who found them," Jarek announced bluntly. Instantly, he wished he could take the words back. Mattie hadn't even told *her* friends, so he *definitely* shouldn't have said anything to Gunner.

Gunner's mouth dropped open. "Ho-ly...the *whole* family?" he asked in disbelief.

Jarek nodded. "Yep. Mother, father, older brother, niece and nephew. The kids were just babies, Gunner, barely three. In fact, the guy was still there when she entered the house. But don't tell anyone, all right? Her best friends don't even know."

Gunner leaned forward and braced his forearms on his knees. If he'd been a dog, his ears would've pricked forward. His green eyes had widened considerably, but remained riveted on Jarek's face.

"Hey, man, her secret's safe with me. So, was she hurt pretty bad?" he questioned in a hushed voice.

"Yeah, she was, and that's all I'm gonna say. Mattie's a really private person and getting information out of her is like pulling teeth," Jarek revealed with a rueful smile.

"So, is she, like, physically scarred?" Gunner probed.

Jarek hesitated, thinking of how to phrase his words so it wouldn't sound like she was deformed.

"She...is, but not so it's noticeable. And it's not as bad as you're thinking. I mean, it was a shock the first time I saw the scars—"

"You *saw* them?" Gunner interjected. "J.T., man, you barely *know* the girl. I can't believe you—"

"Gunner." This time it was Jarek's turn to intercede. He gave his friend a look from under his brows.

"Gunner, *man.* I haven't done anything with Mattie except kiss her. And before you ask, yes it was very enjoyable. I saw the scars by accident," he confided.

Gunner slumped back in his chair as though he'd been rung dry.

"Holy cow. I can't imagine losing my family. I mean, if it were my parents, it would be hard. But Gavin's a different story.

He's my twin, y'know? I don't know what I would do without him," he said in a faint tone.

"I hear you, man," Jarek agreed. "They'd have to put me away for good, cuz I'd probably kill the bastard that ever harmed Kiri."

Gunner shook his head. "Wow. So, who's taking care of her now?"

"A member of her family whom they adopted when she was young. He has his own business, Black Hawk Protection Agency, which specializes in guarding children. His name's Tykota and Mattie refers to him as her Protector. He's Native American, Apache, I think, tall, and can freeze Hell with one glance," Jarek retorted with a snort of laughter.

"Sounds pretty heavy," Gunner commented.

"You don't know the half of it," Jarek returned dryly.

"Was he in the military or something? Cuz you know they probably teach'em little tricks like that," Gunner said.

"He was a Navy SEAL," Jarek confirmed.

Gunner's eyes widened again and he leaned even closer.

"Dude, the stuff those guys see and do is, like, Classified times infinity," he said in wonder. "You talk about pullin' teeth, man, you'd be lucky to get their name, rank, and serial number out of guys like that."

Jarek released another rueful grin. "I kinda got that impression from talking to the guy."

"He must be pretty protective of her," Gunner guessed.

"With a capital P. The wolves are like that, too," Jarek said absently.

Gunner's jaw went slack for the second time. "Did I hear you right? You said wolves, correct?"

"Yep," Jarek nodded.

"Wolves, like, howl-at-the-moon-hunt-in-packs type of wolves?" Gunner clarified.

"Yep."

Gunner leaned back a fraction, cocked his head to one side and gave Jarek a wary look.

"J.T., man, are you sure you should be hangin' with this girl? I mean, she's got Geronimo and a pair of wild animals watchin' over her. How can you even get close to her with all that activity?"

Jarek laughed and shook his head.

"It's not as bad as you think, G. Tykota's a pretty cool guy once you get to know him, and Judah and Dar aren't wild. I mean, not really. They're fifty-fifty, actually, part tame, and part wild. I mean, they'll attack when they're threatened, or if Mattie and Ty are threatened, but once they realize you aren't going to mess with them or their loved ones, they accept you. As for hanging' out with Mattie…" he shrugged a shoulder.

"I like her. I like her a lot. She's different, y'know? She's real, not superficial. She's a straight shooter. No lies, no sugarcoating. Do you know how rare that is in a person?" he paused to shake his head and stare into space.

"And you can't pigeonhole her, either," he went on. "I mean, she's so unpredictable that you can't put her in some category and say she's this or she's that. I never know what she's going to do or say from one moment to the next and I think that's…unique. None of the girls I've ever gone out with have that quality, but that's what makes Mattie so special. That's why I like her."

Gunner studied his friend's expression for a long moment before nodding.

"Okay. Cool," he said quietly. Then he reached out and slapped Jarek's knee. "So what's with the tux?"

"We're doing a routine to Duran Duran's 'A View to a Kill'. Y'know, the theme song from that James Bond movie?" Jarek told him.

CELISE DOWNS

"Oh yeah. I remember the movie, but not the song," Gunner said.

"So what about you, man? You don't look any different than when we go clubbin'", Jarek stated.

Baggy jeans tightly cinched with a slim leather belt, combat boots, and a tight T-shirt was one of the many outfits Jarek had seen Gunner wear on the nights they went out dancing. Come to think of it, *anything* Gunner wore seemed like he was going dancing. He was one of Jarek's best friends and attracted about as much attention from the opposite sex as Jarek did. He was an all-around surf bum reject from Florida. He had a tan that never seemed to fade, short, spiky brown hair that had seen one too many sunny days, blue-green eyes that took on the characteristics of a mood ring, and a blinding white smile that always seemed to say 'Hey brah, I'd rather be surfing.'

He and Gunner shared the same physical build, the same height, and a love of R&B music. Becoming friends had seemed unlikely at the time, but it had been inevitable since they attended the same class at Half-Steppin'. Jarek had known Gunner for almost three years, and looking back, had wondered where Gunner had been when he'd gone though the dancing-is-for-sissies phase of his life. Gunner was a risk taker, had in fact been the one to convince Jarek to join Half-Steppin'. Jarek had yet to regret that decision.

"Hey, J.T, you freakin' out on me? You aren't going to faint are ya?" Gunner's joking brought Jarek out of his reverie.

"No, I'm not going to faint," Jarek grumbled, kicking Gunner on the shin.

"Dude, are you nervous?" he asked.

Jarek scoffed and rolled his eyes. "How many times have we done this, G?"

"Too many."

"I rest my case. So what were you talking about?"

"My partner. She goes to that Catholic school on Central..." Gunner trailed off, snapping his fingers as though he could magically conjure up the right word.

"Shumway?" Jarek supplied.

"Yeah. Shumway. I didn't think they allowed dancing at that place. Anyway, we're doing a routine to music from that Broadway Show 'Stomp'. You ever seen that?" Gunner was saying.

"Oh yeah. They take everyday items like brooms and garbage cans and make music it out if it, right?" Jarek asked.

"Yeah. It's pretty cool. I'd never seen it before until Arlee showed me the video," Gunner said, leaning down to tighten the shoelace on his right boot.

"Huh. I wonder if Mattie would be interested in seeing something like that. She loves ice sk—" Jarek broke off abruptly with a frown. "Who's Arlee?"

"My partner. Arlee Janssen. Definitely not my type," Gunner said with conviction.

Jarek laughed. Gunner preferred athletic girls with a little bit of an edge. Arlee must be kind of shy. He was about to voice that very thought when a tech person opened the door. He no longer had to whistle since the noise level abruptly declined whenever the door opened.

"Okay guys, listen up. We're on a commercial break right now, but after that, couple numbers nine through twelve are up. So when I call your name, and you should already know who you are, step out into the hallway here and wait for your partner. Gunner Simons, Lincoln Seaver, Jamie Zane, and Jarek Thanos," the tech person recited.

Jarek shoved his duffel bag and garment bag into a corner and stood up. Gunner did the same and locked the two together, a procedure their instructor had taught them.

"Showtime, J.T. Good luck to ya, bro," he said, clasping Jarek's hand.

"Right back at ya, G."

CHAPTER THIRTEEN

Friday/Twelve Minus Six

The door to the girls' dressing room opened and a female tech person with a clipboard in her hand stepped in. The girls immediately quieted down.

"Okay, last four of the group, you're up after the commercial break. Arlee Janssen, Rcncc Hathaway, Mataya Black Hawk, and Sabrina Sommerset. Let's go," she said.

The minute Ren heard her name she jumped up and turned anxious eyes to Mattie.

"Oh God," she moaned in a sickly tone. "I hope we're not first."

Mattie stood up, and put a comforting arm around her shoulder as they walked out the door. Whatever she was going to say, however, lodged in her throat the minute she laid eyes on Jarek.

"OhmyGodIthinkI'mgonnafaint," the words came out in a low rush.

"Well, don't expect me to hold you up. I think I'm going to hyperventilate here in about—" Ren's words died abruptly when she followed Mattie's line of vision.

"OhmyGodIthinkI'mgonnafaint," she repeated Mattie's words.

To say that four pairs of eyes nearly bugged out of their sockets was the understatement of the year. And Mattie felt a tad jealous because she knew they weren't bugging out over her. She took a quick peek. *Okay, so maybe* one *pair of eyes was directed at her*, she amended mentally. And it was an added ego boost to notice the sagging jaw line.

Jarek felt his heart lodge itself in his throat, skip beats, then race out of control as he began to walk towards her. It was his Mattie, but not the Mattie he was used to seeing. Her dress covered everything it needed to, like he knew it would, but it hinted at what was beneath. The fire engine red color complimented her dark hair and pale blue eyes. When he held out his hands to her, he was pleased she took them, albeit with a shy smile.

"You look really..." Jarek trailed off and shook his head.

Spreading her arms wide, he ran his eyes up and down her body. At the intense scrutiny, Mattie smiled shyly again and slightly ducked her head. He knew she wasn't used to receiving compliments, or being stared at so blatantly, but Jarek couldn't help himself. He was truly stunned. Floored was actually a more accurate word. Once again she had surprised him. So, once again, he tried to express his thoughts.

"That dress is really..." he trailed off again and shook his head. Again.

Mattie chuckled.

Close, but no cigar, J.T., he scolded himself.

"You're outfit looks totally..."

Jarek rolled his eyes.

Mattie laughed aloud, but still said nothing.

Jarek opened his mouth, probably to stutter again, but he never got the chance.

"What he's trying to say is that you look *extremely* gorgeous. I'm Gunner, by the way. Gunner Simons, J.T.'s best friend. And you must be Mattie," Gunner stepped in, pushing Jarek to one side.

Mattie laughed again and took the proffered hand after a momentary hesitation. She didn't know what to make of Jarek's friend. He hadn't told her anything about his friends. Then again, she hadn't said much about *her* friends, either. Flashing a bemused glance at Jarek, Mattie thought they were going to have to remedy that situation very soon.

"Don't mean to shake hands and run, but the commercial break's almost over and they've been trying to hustle us to the stage," Gunner was saying.

At that, Jarek seemed to snap out of whatever spell he'd been under and grabbed Mattie's hand.

"C'mon, we'd better get going. I don't know what the lineup is, but I sure hope we're not first," he said, practically dragging her behind him.

Mattie easily kept up with his quick stride and beamed widely. "Funny you should mention that. Ren said the same thing a few minutes ago."

"Ren. That wouldn't happen to be the girl my best friend is currently salivating over, would it?" Jarek asked with a quick glance over his shoulder.

"You'd be salivating too if I was wearing that little scrap of nothing," Mattie accused with a light pinch.

"Guilty," Jarek shot back, laughing when she lightly punched his arm. "By the way, you *do* look extremely gorgeous," he added in a husky tone.

"Well, I'd have to say ditto for you, too, Mr. Bond," she intoned in a British accent.

"Are you nervous at all?" he asked.

"A little, I guess. I've never done something of this magnitude before. You?" Mattie reciprocated.

"I'd have to agree with you on that. My dance instructor tries to prepare us for things like this, y'know? I don't think you can ever really be prepared, though."

They were standing in the wings now. Pepe and Sophie were standing on the wide, three-tiered risers, pretending to have a sword fight with their microphones. Mattie shook her head and chuckled lowly under her breath.

CELISE DOWNS

"Kids. They act just like kids," she murmured.

"I know," Jarek said in amusement.

"I thought that whole act was just for show, but it's not. They really do act like that behind the cameras," she said in awe.

"Amazing," Jarek retorted.

Mattie continued to watch the couple as the music queued up and they were once again the hosts of *Dance Jam Productions.* She was also aware of the nervous shuffling going on around her. *Or maybe it was tension brought on by the explosive impact of Ren's outfit,* she thought with a half smile. As it turned out, she and Jarek would go last, Gunner and his partner third, Ren and Jamie second.

The stagehands had put the remaining four couples at separate points on the sidelines, so they could enter and exit without colliding with one another. Mattie and Jarek had a view of Pepe and Sophie from behind and slightly to the right. Mattie was perfectly content with this arrangement. It gave her the opportunity to bring up something they needed to talk about.

"You heard about the party tomorrow night?" she asked in a low tone, her eyes on the hosts.

"...so without further ado, here's couple number nine, Sabrina Sommerset and Lincoln Seaver dancing to Coolio's 'Gangstas Paradise' from the *Dangerous Minds* Soundtrack," Pepe announced.

"I heard," Jarek replied.

"If anything happens, it'll happen there," she said.

Jarek raised their joined hands to his mouth and kissed her knuckles. He stared down at her for a long moment, searching every feature of her face before connecting with her ice blue eyes.

"You're worried about Ren".

Mattie's eyebrows shot up. *Well,* that *had certainly come from left field.*

"A little, I guess. Whether she becomes a regular or not, she's still invited to that party tomorrow night. She can handle herself. I made sure of that. And I told her we should stick together and get our own drinks," she said.

Jarek nodded. "That sounds like a good plan."

Mattie leaned her head against his biceps. As she watched the couple walk off the floor, she felt Jarek kiss the top of her head. She raised her head to look at him, then reached up with her free hand to caress his cheek. Jarek leaned down towards her, intent on kissing her, but paused mere inches from her lips.

"You're missing Ren's performance," he whispered.

"That's okay. I'm recording from home," she whispered back.

Jarek closed the distance and gently pressed his mouth against hers. Framing her face in his hands, he softly stroked her lips with his before moving on to nuzzle the side of her neck. With one last peck on each cheek, he leaned back slightly to look at her. Mattie reached up and wiped away traces of her lipstick with her thumb.

"What was that for?" she asked in a breathless tone.

Jarek rubbed his lips together and Mattie automatically mimicked the gesture, knowing he had probably smeared her lipstick. She hoped she didn't look like a clown.

"For luck. And because you look so gorgeous today," Jarek shrugged, his gaze riveted on her face. "Mainly because I was tempted. You are a very tempting young woman, Ms. Black Hawk," he added in a low tone. He kissed her on the forehead then pulled her into a light embrace.

"What are you planning on doing after this?" he asked.

Mattie shrugged, carefully placing her head on his chest without messing up her hair.

"I'm not sure yet. I need to work on my routine for the studio's dance concert. And Ren had said something about wanting to—" she broke off abruptly and straightened as her eyes landed on her friend.

Ren and her partner, Jamie, were standing in the wings. It looked like she was mad. Blazing mad. And taking a nice big strip out of Jamie's hide.

"What's happening over there?" Jarek asked, narrowing his eyes.

"I dunno, but I have the feeling we missed something," Mattie answered absently, her eyes never leaving the arguing couple.

She could hear Ren's voice now. The angrier she got, the thicker her accent became. By the look of her staccato movements, she was probably incomprehensible by now. Mattie watched as Ren made a move to walk away, but Jamie reached out to grab her wrist. Mattie tensed instantly and took a step forward. Jarek stopped her.

"Don't. She can handle it. You said she could, remember? And if she can't, Gunner will get to her before you will," he said.

Jarek was right. With her free hand, Ren reached out and clasped Jamie's neck. At the same time, she hooked her right leg around his, sweeping it out from under him. In a matter of seconds, Jamie Zane was flat on his back with Ren literally in his face.

"Damn," Jarek whispered in awe. "Where'd she learn to do *that*?"

"Me," Mattie announced with smug pride.

Gunner and his partner left the floor and Pepe and Sophie took their place. Jarek knew his friend had seen the confrontation between the couple, and got the distinct feeling that he'd been going through the motions for the rest of his routine. Gunner came from the same family values background as Jarek, where manhandling a female was definitely not tolerated. Jarek hoped that Jamie would make a run for the door, because Gunner would have something to say. And only about fifty percent would be verbal.

Jarek smiled and squeezed her hand. "Are you ready?"

Mattie smiled back in return. "Yep."

"Nervous?"

"You already asked me that."

Jarek's smiled sheepishly. "Yeah, guess I did."

Mattie chuckled and watched Sophie and Pepe.

"It's going to be a tough decision for the judges," he said.

"No doubt," Sophie agreed. "Well, we're down to our final contestants."

"For those of you just tuning in to today's episode, *Dance Jam* had a contest last weekend at Sun Devil Stadium."

"Yep. DJP is looking for new blood," Pepe added.

Mattie and Jarek visibly winced at the words.

"Hundreds of people showed up to shake their groove thang-"

"—And out of those hundreds, we chose twelve finalists," Sophie supplied.

"Now, those finalists had to create a dance routine to the music from a movie soundtrack of their choice—"

"—And that's what you all are viewing today. From today's crop of finalists, our special panel of dance experts is going to choose six couples for the final stage tomorrow. The Copycat Round," Pepe announced dramatically.

"In dance lingo, that means DJP regulars are going to teach a dance routine and we're going to see how well the finalists keep up," Sophie explained.

"Yeah. That'll be the *true* test of a DJP regular. They all make it look easy, but it takes practice, practice, practice," Pepe singsonged.

"And now, our final couple."

"She's a senior at Catalina Valley High—"

"—And *he's* a senior at Lakeview High—"

"—So if you're a fan of James Bond—"

"—And the James Bond women—"

"—Then you'll love our final contestants."

"Here's Mataya Black Hawk—"

"—And Jarek Thanos, mixin' us a little martini—"

"—Shaken, not stirred—" Sophie intoned in an exaggerated British accent.

"—With Duran Duran's 'A View to a Kill'", they announced in unison.

Jarek released Mattie's hand and swaggered on stage by himself while she waited for her cue. When Jarek froze facing the camera, it was her turn to appear. Slinking her way on stage, she circled him slowly, seductively, dragging her fingers across his chest and back as she did so.

Matching him smoldering stare for smoldering stare, sexy smile for sexy smile, Mattie came to a stop behind his left shoulder. Looking directly into the camera lens, she let her smile grow slowly as she cocked her left eyebrow and raised her chin. Mattie then slid her gaze to Jarek's profile and slid her hands up his back and over his shoulders. She slowly drew his jacket down his arms and then tossed it over her own shoulder, letting it dangle off her index finger.

She made a move to turn away, but knew Jarek would stop her. He hastily divested himself of the toy gun and just as quickly grabbed the tail of his jacket, using it as leverage to draw her closer. Jarek threw his jacket aside then dipped her twice in rapid succession, right in sync with the dramatic music.

They looked at one another, noses almost touching, then turned their heads to the camera in unison. And then the song began...

"Whew, we've got some potential DJP regulars here, Soph," Pepe said with pronounced glee.

"I'd have to agree with you on that one, Pep. I definitely wouldn't want to be a judge right now," she countered.

"Well, let's bring all twelve couples back out here and see if the experts agree with the people at home," Pepe said with a sweep of his arm.

As Mattie and Jarek walked onto the floor, she managed to jockey a position next to Ren. She grasped her friend's hand and squeezed it, all the while probing her face. Something was definitely wrong. Ren was smiling, but it was strained. And she never once glanced in Jamie's direction, who was standing on her other side. Mattie didn't want to look at him, either. She was afraid Jarek might end up pulling her off of the guy.

She was glad Ren had defended herself, but it shouldn't have been necessary in the first place. *What had Jamie done?* She wondered. She was anxious to find out. Since she and Ren had ridden in together, she had a feeling she was going to get an earful on the way home. Or maybe she'd get lucky and find out after the show. Mattie glanced up at Jarek, smiled at him, then moved her gaze beyond him to Gunner. He was wearing the same expression as Ren. He kept shifting his weight and curling and uncurling his hands. *Had he seen what happened?* She wondered again with a slight frown. He must have because it looked like he wanted to punch something. Or someone.

When Mattie raised her eyes again to Jarek, she caught him staring at her. She smiled again, but the excitement had waned. He seemed to sense that and gently squeezed her hand. There was a questioning look in his green eyes but she couldn't say anything. At that moment, a DJP regular strode onto the stage and handed Pepe a folded piece of paper. The dancer immediately left but not before waving to the camera and the live audience.

"Okay, the dance experts have made their decision. But before we announce the winners, let's give our twelve finalists a big round of applause," Pepe suggested, tucking his mike under his armpit to clap his hands.

Sophie did the same with hers, but turned to look at the finalists as she did so. Mattie smiled back cheekily and dropped into a light curtsy. Sophie laughed then turned around to face the camera.

"Whoever gets chosen today will be invited back tomorrow for the Copycat Round," she said.

"But there are no losers today because all twelve finalists will be invited to a special VIP party—"

"—In their honor—"

"—At Club Cabana. They'll be able to get up close and personal with the DJP dancers-"

"—And bust a move for the rest of the night when the doors are opened to the public," Sophie concluded.

"So heeeeeerrrre we go. The six finalists are..."

Mattie and Jarek tensed up as the two hosts took turns reading off names.

"...Couple Number Twelve, Mataya Black Hawk and Jarek Thanos..."

Ren screamed and threw her arms around Mattie's neck. Mattie was doing a pretty good impression of Mariah Carey herself as she returned her friend's exuberant hug. When Ren finally released her, Mattie turned to Jarek. A huge smile creased his face as he enveloped her in a tight embrace. He let out a joyous whoop and lifted her over his head. Holding her arms out, Mattie dropped her head back and laughed aloud. It was a good laugh. A laugh that started deep. A laugh that had been waiting to be released for ten years.

At the door to the girl's dressing room, Jarek leaned down and gave Mattie a lingering kiss. The kind he'd wanted to give her before their performance.

"I'm really glad you're my partner," he murmured against her lips.

"Not as glad as I am that you're *my* partner," she whispered back.

"I'll meet you back out here?" he inquired.

"Yep."

"You going to change?"

"Definitely. I feel much too exposed in this outfit," she confessed.

Jarek ran a fingertip over her cheek. "Did I mention how gorgeous you look in that dress?" he asked in a low tone.

Mattie gave him a tremulous smile. "Yes, you did."

Nodding in satisfaction, he leaned down and kissed her again.

"I'll see you in a few." With another quick peck to her cheek, he was gone.

In the dressing room, Mattie found a suitably clothed Ren facing the mirror, reapplying her make-up. Dressed in long, baggy shorts, tennis shoes, and an army camouflage tank top, Ren was back in skater chick mode. The heavy stage appearance was being removed to make room for the natural one that Ren preferred, but she'd left her hair alone. She caught Mattie's eye in the mirror and gave her a huge smile.

"God, I'm happy for y'all, Mattie," she drawled.

"Thanks. Jay and I are pretty ecstatic about it, too," Mattie replied.

She untied her shoes, stepped out of them, and dug around in her duffel bag for the clothes she'd put on that morning. All the while, she was flashing surreptitious glances at Ren. After changing in a bathroom stall and washing her face, Mattie sat next to her friend and began to redo her own make-up. For the next few minutes, the girls remained silent as they concentrated on getting ready. Fifteen minutes later, the room was almost empty. Mattie couldn't wait any longer.

"You want to tell me what happened out there?"

Ren sighed, rolled her eyes, and tossed down her mascara wand. Crossing her arms over her chest, she shook her head. Her eyes had yet to connect with Mattie's. Mattie knew before she even opened her mouth that Ren was going to let loose with a down-home Southern accent. And she wasn't disappointed.

"Jarek's friend, y'know Gunner? He made a comment about my appearance. Nothing' offensive," she hurriedly assured when Mattie was about to protest.

"It wasn't mean at all. It was quite flattering' in fact, but Jamie went *postal* on me in some sadistic...possessive...boyfriend' type of mode. He then proceeded to ruin my chances of ever dancing' on DJP again without having' to hang my head in complete and utter shame."

Mattie swallowed back a laugh at her friend's theatrics. She was up and pacing the floor, waving her hands expressively in the air. Her accent was becoming as thick as a milkshake, and her anger was almost out of control. *When she gets her panties in a crunch, they really come out wrinkled,* Mattie thought as she sat back to watch the show that was Renee Hathaway. Gunner should get a look at her now. If he liked her before, he'd *really* like her now.

"So what'd he do?" Mattie wanted to know.

"You didn't see it? Geez, the whole frickin' *state* saw it," she ranted on.

178

"No, I missed it. I'm sorry. So what did he do?" Mattie pressed.

"Oh, a bunch of things. He tripped me up during some turns, nearly dropped me during our lift, and practically *shoved* me out of the camera frame at the end. He was getting' back at me for what Gunner said, I swear," she accused with narrowed eyes. "An' then he had the nerve to try an' manhandle me as I was walking' off stage." Ren kicked a chair leg.

Suddenly, she stopped mid-pace, turned to Mattie and gave her the most devilish smile Mattie had ever seen.

"I'm thinking' all those karate lessons with you are paying' off, Mattie," she said in obvious glee.

"I noticed," Mattie retorted dryly.

"Did I do good, darlin'?"

Mattie let out a bark of laughter. "You did great, *darlin'*. Just like I taught you."

Ren calmed down enough to reclaim the chair she'd vacated earlier. Mattie blinked in awe, wondering when the firemen had come to douse the fire. One minute she was a pissed off skater chick, and barely two minutes later, she was her usual self.

"If I'd had my board I would've clocked him with it," she muttered, slouching in her chair.

Mattie laughed."I would've paid to see that. But you know, Mici did warn you about those college guys," she pointed out.

"So she did. Next time I'll listen. Better yet, I'll avoid them altogether until *I'm* in college," Ren decided.

"Good idea."

CHAPTER FOURTEEN

Saturday/Copy Cat Round

On Saturday morning, Mattie felt a keen sense of déjà vu. When she and Tykota stepped into the backyard to perform their daily routine, the weather felt the same way it had approximately a week ago. The day she had come face to face with Jarek Thanos. The day they had become finalists at the Dance Jam Productions contest. Mattie followed Tykota to the mowed out spot near The Memory Tree. Positioning herself slightly behind and to the left of him, she began to warm up. A few minutes later, they were ready to start. Although she was usually able to clear her mind during the morning ritual, she wasn't able to today.

She would need to leave for the studio in an hour or two and she had yet to talk to Tykota about his assignment. She kept telling Jarek that it would be over by tonight, but she couldn't be sure. His assignments had a tendency to last for months on end, sometimes for years. She prayed it wouldn't drag out that long. Twenty minutes later, Mattie matched her steps with Tykota's as they walked back to the house, Dar and Judah flanking them on either side.

"You have been very quiet," Tykota observed in his familiar soft voice.

"Mmm. Just thinking," she murmured.

"About what?"

"This current assignment of yours. I'm torn. I don't know if I should back out, if I should continue. And then there's Ren. She's so excited about this whole party thing happening tonight. Something like this should be fun, for the both of us. But all I can do is worry," Mattie admitted in a troubled tone.

Tykota put a hand on her shoulder to stop her. Turning her so they were face to face, he caressed the back of her head.

"You know I would not let anything happen to you," he stated.

"I know," Mattie nodded.

"If I thought you would be in danger, I would have made you drop out a long time ago."

Mattie nodded again. "I know," she repeated.

"You will not be there alone, sweetling. I would never allow that to happen. It is fortunate that Renee is not going with her dance partner," he said.

Mattie turned her head to the side and looked at him out of the corner of her eye.

"How so?"

"Because Ramsey will escort her instead," he claimed.

Mattie laughed and shook her head. "She'll *love* that. Ram's definitely a major step up from that college creep. I wish you could've seen her lay him out, Ty. You would've been proud."

Tykota nodded sagely. "I am sure I would have been. So what is troubling you still, sweetling?"

Mattie turned away and started walking again.

"Mici predicted this. She did a reading and told us that there was a black cloud over this contest, that something wasn't right. She said that Ren was not really a part of it, but that I would be. Lo and behold, I'm in it pretty deep. How deep, you ask? Enough to know that I should be wearing rubber boots that reach my waist," her voice rose at the end. "And no matter *what* happens, win or lose, this whole experience has been ruined for me. What should've been a fun and enjoyable opportunity has turned into one big ball of worry and speculation. My opinions and...and *views* of the show will forever be tainted. And it's all because of your damned assignment."

Mattie slammed a fist on her leg. Judah whined in concern.

CELISE DOWNS

"I wish with all my heart you that hadn't told me anything. I wish you had just treated me like all your other clients and done your job." She wiped away tears that had fallen down her face without her notice. Tykota blocked her path and took both shoulders in his hands to stop her.

"It is because you are not a client that I had to tell you, Mataya. You are family. *My* family, not some assignment," he said with quiet intensity.

"The first two times, you were a defenseless child. I could not tell you what was happening because you would have not understood. You had been traumatized. But circumstances are different now. You are older, better prepared, and you understand. I could not have kept you in the dark about something like this. You never would have forgiven me for keeping it from you."

Mattie sighed and closed her eyes, knowing he was right. And at that moment, all the fight went out of her. Her feelings had reached the boiling point and thank God Tykota had let her bubble over.

"I know. I *know* all of this," she whispered, "but if this is what your job is all about, then I don't want any part of it."

She looked up at Tykota with sad eyes. "I can't do what you do, Ty. I can't do...*this.* I know you created the Agency because of me, but when you're gone, someone else is going to have to run it. I'm sorry, Ty, but I wasn't born to be a guardian," she entreated.

Tykota caressed her face with his hand, pulled her against him.

"No. You were born to be something else."

***

182

"Welcome to another edition of Dance Jam Productions, where the beats don't stop and the music's hot. We're your hosts, Sophie Brown—"

"—And Pepe Carrington. We're soooo glad you all could join us today—"

"—Because today is our last and final round in the Dance Jam Productions Dance Contest," Sophie jumped in.

"If you missed yesterday's show..." Pepe paused dramatically, "well, then you're S.O.L. unless one of your friends taped it."

"That's harsh, Pep," Sophie laughed. "But it doesn't matter if you missed yesterday's show because today is the day you wanna see, anyway."

"Sure is, Soph. We've got six couples, from different high schools all over the valley, vying for three open spots on our DJP Dance Team," Pepe explained.

"It's the Copy Cat Round and we're gonna see how well the couples are at dance instruction—"

"So don't touch that dial. We'll be right back after these messages."

***

"Hey, your phone's ringin', man," a DJP dancer handed the cell phone to the young man.

"Thanks," he said, reaching out for it. "Yeah?" he rapped out.

"Club Cabana. Never would've thought of that place."

The voice was different this time. Deep, well modulated, with a hint of patronization. This wasn't the same person that usually called him. This was a voice he recognized, for he'd heard it all his life. A voice he hadn't heard in a long time and

183

had hoped never to hear again. Eyes darting quickly in every direction, the young man made his way to a darkened corridor. Making sure he was alone, he took a couple of deep breaths to calm his racing heart.

"How did you get this number?"

"I'm your father. I know everything about you. Just because I don't call much, doesn't mean I don't know how to keep tabs on you."

"What do you want?"

"I just wanted to tell you how pleased I am about the upcoming contributions. I have some needy...patients anxiously waiting for new lives. I've been thinking about turning over the business—"

"I don't want your damn business," the young man interrupted scathingly. "I told your lackey that this is the last time and now I'm telling *you*. This is the *very* last time."

"You're lucky to be alive, my boy," the voice intoned silkily. "You mustn't forget how you got where you are today, because I won't let you. Ever."

Click.

***

"We're back! This is Dance Jam Productions—"

"—And we're your hosts, Sophie Brown—"

"—And Pepe Carrington. You're watching a special edition of DJP because today is the day we're going to welcome six new people into our family."

"We sure are, Pep. It's time for the Copy Cat Round—"

"—The final phase of our DJP Contest," Pepe dodged in.

"While you viewers were hearin' the latest music news—"

"—And watchin' the newest videos—"

"—Our six couples were having a dance lesson," Sophie said with a beaming smile.

"Yuh-huh. So for the next hour, you're gonna see different snippets of dance routines—"

"—Taught to them by DJP regulars who volunteered their time—"

"—And performed to various musical artists," Pepe finished.

"Of course, in between all that, we're still gonna have our music news—"

"—Movie reviews—"

"—Video playbacks—"

"—DJP Dance Break—"

"—DJP Dance *Lesson*—"

"—And plenty of time to shake your groove thang—"

"—Bust a move—"

"—Get your dancey-dance on—"

"Turn yourself loose like a long-nec—"

"O-*kay*, Pep, I think our viewers get the message," Sophie interrupted dryly, with a pointed look at her cohort.

Pepe cocked his thumb and pointed his trigger finger at the camera, then winked and flashed a crooked grin as he made a clicking sound.

"You are so right, partner. The point is, by the end of the show, you will know what three couples are going to become our new DJP Regulars," he explained.

"So let's get this show on the road, because I know our couples are getting' a little antsy back there," Sophie said with a raised eyebrow in question, nodding her head.

"I know I would be. Is our first couple ready?" Pepe called out, looking beyond the camera's view. After getting confirmation, he went on.

"Aw-*right*! He's a junior at A.G. Case—"

"-And she's a junior at Halloran. Here's couple number one—"

"—*Risa Cage and Marcus Sangne*," they shouted simultaneously before running off stage.

And so it went. Between video breaks, commercials, and music news, six couples performed their given routine, each hoping to become a part of the DJP family. Mattie was beyond antsy and coming up on irritated. They would let two couples dance in a row before going to a commercial. Once the show resumed, they would let the studio audience get out on the floor and dance for a while. Watching everyone dance made Mattie want to get out there and dance, too, but she knew she couldn't. She didn't even dare do it on the sidelines. The contestants weren't allowed. If it weren't for Jarek's presence, she would've gone crazy.

"You all right?" he asked, coming up behind her and wrapping his arms around her waist.

Mattie folded her arms over his and leaned back against him, never taking her eyes off the crush of writhing bodies.

"Yeah." Her answer came out on a sigh.

"I was talking to Gunner when I looked over and saw you swingin' your hips. I thought I'd come over and hold you back," he teased, nipping the fleshy lobe of her ear.

Mattie chuckled, not even realizing she'd been moving. "It's definitely tempting, let me tell you. All this waiting they're making us go through is ridiculous."

"Well, the show *is* supposed to be for an hour, you know. It doesn't take an hour for six couples to dance, so they have to fill the time up with something," Jarek explained logically.

"I know. It's just…I don't see why we have to be subjected to this kind of temptation. I mean, why couldn't they have made us wait in the dressing room until it was our turn?" Mattie complained.

Mattie felt more than saw Jarek shrug.

"To torture us, I guess," he retorted.

"*I'll* say," Mattie grumbled under her breath. "It doesn't help any that they're playing' some good stuff."

"Well, hey, at least Caid and Jana picked some good stuff for us, too," Jarek pointed out with a squeeze to her waist.

"Yes they did," she murmured, her thoughts going to the regulars who had taught them their routine.

Jarek sighed, rested his chin on her shoulder and pulled her tighter against his chest. He watched the dancers for a moment before clearing his throat.

"Have you talked to Ty lately?" he asked.

"This morning, actually," Mattie admitted.

Jarek lifted his head to look down at her. "Really? So, what did he have to say?"

"Well, he's pretty sure something's going to happen tonight. It would be the perfect opportunity. Big crowd, plenty of victims, no one's really going to notice anything suspicious until it's too late. But not just anybody can walk in off the street for this party. They're going to have to secure it somehow. Invitations, a guest list, a special wristband, bouncers at the door, something," Mattie explained.

"So he has a plan, right?"

"Yep. Ramsey."

Jarek blinked in confusion, turning her around to face him. "Who's Ramsey? And what can he do that Ty can't?"

"He's one of Ty's guys. They served together on the same SEAL unit. And he'll be escorting Ren to the party since she refuses to go with the College Creep," Mattie said.

Jarek's lips twitched at that last part. He didn't blame the girls, really, for he was sure Mattie had wanted to do something far worse. He opened his mouth to ask something else, but never got the chance. A tech person was ushering them onto the floor, and before they knew it, their chosen song was playing. At the end of the show, the winners had been announced. Jarek Thanos and Mataya Black Hawk were going to show up at the party that night. As regulars on *Dance Jam Productions.*

CHAPTER FIFTEEN

Saturday Night/Culprit Caught

After a day at the spa, courtesy of Ty and the guys, Mattie and Ren were back at the house getting ready for the party. Once she made sure Ren was comfortably set up in the guest room, Mattie went to her own room and pulled her outfit from the closet. She didn't realize how tense she'd been this past week until her muscles had been massaged into liquid. She'd had to practically crawl off the table she'd felt so relaxed. It had been exactly what she'd needed, without even knowing it, and she'd thanked Ty repeatedly. No, wait. That had been Ren. *She'd* hugged him to death. Repeatedly. At five-thirty, Mattie studied herself in the full-length mirror. The black ribbon-trimmed stretch lace dress skimmed down her body to fall just past her knees. Lined in light pink, the sleeves were off the shoulder and had a flattering bunching effect in the bodice. The minute she'd seen it in a Frederick's of Hollywood catalogue, she'd had to have it. It wasn't her usual style, a little more daring in the chest area, but she didn't have to worry about her scars showing. And it had reminded her of something Marilyn Monroe would wear while breathily serenading her admirers in a smoky nightclub.

A black beaded cross necklace circled her throat, four black beaded stretch bracelets tinkled merrily on her right wrist, and black strappy high heels encased her feet. In that same catalogue, she'd found a cute black and pink mini corset handbag with a mesh overlay that had gone perfectly with her outfit.

With one last pat to her hair, a sleek upswept topknot with tendrils framing her face and neck, Mattie went to check on Ren.

"Wow, you look great, Mattie," Ren gushed upon seeing her friend.

"Look who's talking, girlio," Mattie praised, taking hold of Ren's hands and spreading their arms wide. "Yowza, yowza. I hope Ty doesn't make you go home and change," she joked.

To say that Ren looked like she was dressed to kill was the understatement of the year. Once Jamie set eyes on her, he was going to wish he hadn't messed up. A black pleather mini skirt and black corset top with pink ribbons crisscrossing the front molded her body. Two-tone pink four-inch heels with ankle straps clung to her feet, and a Swarovski crystal choker proclaiming she was "SEXY" bling-blinged at her neck. Her hair had been attacked with Bed Hed products, giving her that rumpled look, and a pink satin corset handbag adorned with four tiny black bows dangled from one hand.

Ren had found her whole outfit in the same Frederick's catalogue as well. Mattie thought they complimented one another quite well, even though the black and pink color scheme had been accidental. They both were fully aware that if anything took place tonight as expected, there would be no dancing later on. In fact, Club Cabana would probably end up being closed down for the night. But Ren had wanted to make a lasting impression. On Chris Morrow, no doubt.

"C'mon," Mattie urged. "All of the guys are here. I don't want to leave Jarek out there by himself for too long."

Her worries proved unfounded moments later when they walked into a room full of laughing males.

"I can see they're really giving him a hard time," Ren joked under her breath.

Mattie poked her in the ribs with her elbow, her eyes never leaving the roomful of men. She felt the sting of emotion at seeing Ty's friends together. She couldn't remember the last time they'd all been in one room for more than a day. Mattie had felt like she was going to the prom when Ramsey and Jarek had asked her the color of their dresses. "So we can match," Ramsey had said. Mattie didn't have to look at Ren to know that her jaw was swinging near the floor. Her own had promptly dropped down and had sustained rug burns the moment she'd laid eyes on their escorts.

Both men wore black slacks and dress shoes, but there the similarities ended. Ramsey's short-sleeved shirt was made of a shimmery spandex material that stretched across a well-muscled torso and biceps. He worked out on a regular basis and it showed; the shirt outlined his V-cut shape to perfection. The deep red color and his shoulder-length wavy brown hair sleeked back in a ponytail made his round blue eyes appear even brighter.

"Holy splintered skateboards, Batgirl. I'm going on a date with Lorenzo Lamas. God, I wish I was almost thirty," Ren groaned with a heartfelt sigh.

Mattie's gaze took in Jarek's coal black hair swinging freely, and the short-sleeved button down shirt in dark blue satin. The color made his eyes an emerald green and they shone with inner mirth as he listened to something Heath was saying.

"And I'm going on a date with Pierce Brosnan's son. And he's the same age as me. Go figure," she taunted back with a cavalier shrug.

"Brat," Ren hissed, smacking Mattie's arm with the back of her hand.

It was then that Tykota noticed them and surged to his feet. The others followed suit.

"You both look incredibly beautiful," he said huskily in his native tongue.

"Amen to that."

"Ditto."

"Absolutely stunning."

"Gorgeous."

"Jiminy Cry, I'm going to have to beat'em off with a stick tonight."

"Totally hot." This from Jarek.

"Thank you," Mattie and Ren said in unison.

They received hugs and kisses all round before Tykota clapped his hands to get their attention.

"All right, you guys. Get moving," he said. "Let's put this guy out of commission."

***

Mattie, Jarek, Ramsey, and Ren arrived at Club Cabana shortly after seven. They were greeted by a burly bouncer and an elegantly dressed Sophie Brown, who told them to sit at the Dancer's Table. The other regulars had yet to show up, but Gunner and his partner, Arlee, were occupying two seats. Mattie thought she looked very pretty in her flirty red chiffon dress with it's white polka dots, ruffled cap sleeves, drape-front bustline, and slight A-line flare. And Ren had raved about her black patent leather three and a half inch Mary Jane pumps.

"I'm going to the bar," Ramsey announced after seating Ren. "Anybody want anything?"

Requests came from around the table and Jarek went with him to help. For the next two hours, they ate from a buffet that was constantly replenished, danced, and socialized. The special VIP party was almost over and the club would be opening to the public soon. Mattie was having such a good time, as was Jarek, that she'd nearly forgotten the problems at hand. But she was just about to be reminded.

After dancing to a particularly fast song, Jarek, Mattie, Ren and Ramsey went back to the table. Arlee and Gunner had made the cut as well, and it was clear she had a serious love jones for her dance partner. But shoulder-length brown hair in spiral curls, sparkling green eyes and a wicked red slash across the lips couldn't hold a candle to Ren's Knock'em-Out-In-Twenty-Paces outfit.

Poor girl, Mattie thought. She was getting to know Gunner pretty well this evening and it was apparent that Ren was more his flavor. There was some subtle flirting going on, not that Ren had noticed. She'd managed to garner the attention of her beloved Chris Morrow and was currently playing hard to get with the utmost glee. It was funny really, because Ramsey was making it even harder by portraying the overprotective "friend."

Mattie took a long pull from her bottled water, fanning a hand in front of her face at the same time.

"I need to go freshen up, cool off....something," she panted.

"Yeah, me too. C'mon," Ren agreed, picking up her purse. "What about you, Arlee?"

Flicking a glance at Gunner, the girl pasted on a smile so fake, Mattie wondered if it hurt. *Guys can be so dumb....and clueless,* she thought.

"No, you two go ahead. I think I'm going to get some more fruit from the buffet table," Arlee replied.

"Okay, we'll be back in a minute," Mattie said, snatching up her own purse.

The two girls strolled down the dimly lit corridor to the women's bathroom.

"Ick. It's not much better in here," Ren said with a twist of her lips.

She was right. Mattie was so hot she was starting to feel sticky, and a smoke cloud hovered near the ceiling. She glanced around to find no windows...and two small air vents. Which were probably just for show.

"No wonder it's so hot in here," Mattie murmured in disgust. "I don't know why they couldn't have held this party at Club Avatar. They film the show there. They could've had the same set up. Not to mention better facilities."

"Who knows? Who cares? I've got two guys fighting for my attention," Ren boasted, picking up a couple of paper towels and dousing them with cold water.

Mattie followed suit, wanting to get out of the stifling room as quickly as possible. "Gunner the Daredevil or Chris the Dancer? Which one will she choose? Find out next week on...*Thrasher Girl*," she intoned in a dramatic announcer's voice.

Ren let out an affronted gasp and threw one of her soggy paper towels at Mattie. Mattie sidestepped it easily, watching it fall to the floor with a splat.

"Nasty, traitorous bitch," Ren said, laughing. "Besides, my choice is a no-brainer. Chris is gay," she added.

Mattie's eyes widened in shock, then she ducked down to check out the stalls. Empty, thank God. She straightened back up and stared at Ren. For the second time that night? Mattie felt her jaw drop.

"*Shut...up*. Are you *serious?* Chris Morrow. DJP regular? The guy you've been drooling over for the past year? He's *gay?*" she asked in disbelief.

"Yep," Ren sighed, patting her forehead and neck with the other damp towel.

"Are you sure?"

"Positive," Ren said, taking her compact out and flipping it open.

"But...how?"

Ren released a snort of laughter. "He loved my outfit. Raved about it, in fact. He wanted to know if I made the corset myself or if it was from one of the design houses. The man knows fashion, Mattie. More than I'll *ever* care to know, thank you very much."

Mattie was flummoxed. "B-but he's been practically salivating over you, flirting with you—"

"It may *seem* like flirting to you, honeychile', but believe me, it's not," Ren drawled around the make-up pad she was patting on her face. "I inspired him. The guy wanted to give me an award for best dressed, he was so inspired. The flirting you think you're seein' is not flirtin', but courtin'."

Mattie frowned, leaning her hip against the counter. "Courting. Uh-huh. For what, exactly?"

"He wants me to be his live mannequin. Be his lead model to showcase his stuff at fashion shows. According to him, I'm the perfect body type for his clothes," Ren explained, closing her compact with a snap and tossing it in her purse.

"I've been laughing in his face all night because I've been telling him this is a one-shot deal. I normally don't dress like this. You know that. Not even when we used to go out dancing. Who the hell can dance in a mini-skirt and heels that are going to leave my feet screaming in pain later on, anyway? Not me. He didn't believe me when I told him that when I grow up, I wanna be just like Tony Hawk. I told him he was lucky...I left my skateboard at home." Ren shook her head as if to say "Poor guy. He doesn't know when to give up."

Mattie laughed in disbelief. As far as she was concerned, Chris Morrow was spitting in the wind. Ren practically lived in baggy cargo pants and long board shorts. On the off chance that she wore a skirt, mini or otherwise, she paired it with combat boots, Converse, or Vans. If Chris ever saw her like that, he'd slap a fashion citation on her butt and run like hell.

"So, does anyone else know? The other dancers? Sophie and Pepe? The general public?" Mattie asked.

Ren rummaged through her purse and pulled out a tube of lipstick. She was in the process of uncapping it when two girls breezed in. She glanced at them as she leaned closer to the mirror.

"Everyone else but the general public," she replied nonchalantly, then quickly followed up with, "I can't believe you and Jarek made it in. That's so awesome."

Mattie followed her lead. "Yeah. I think I'm still in shock."

"Gunner's pretty cool, too. Did you know he likes to skateboard, too?" Ren said, recapping her lipstick and tossing it back in her purse.

"Really? No, I didn't know that. So you guys have something in common, sounds like, " Mattie commented, trying to fluff up the limp strands of hair dangling on her neck.

"Totally. He thinks it's wild that a girl likes skateboarding. He says he doesn't see any at the skate park he goes to," Ren said, then held up a finger. "Let me rephrase that. He *does* see girls at the skate park. But they're only there to check out the view. Board Bunnies, if you will."

"Maybe you should invite him to the one *you* go to," Mattie suggested.

"I already did," Ren answered with a sly smile. "I gotta use the bathroom, then I'll be ready."

"Okay. I'll just wait for you in the hall. It's too hot in here," Mattie said, opening the door.

"Coolbeans. I'll be right out," Ren said, before disappearing into a stall.

Stepping outside, Mattie leaned against the wall and breathed a sigh of relief at the feel of a slight breeze wafting over her skin. The two girls, who had walked in earlier, strode past her and congratulated her on becoming a regular. Mattie thanked them, feeling the cool breeze once again. It was coming from a door that was standing ajar at the end of the corridor. Glancing in that direction, she quickly flattened herself against the wall, trying to blend in with the shadows, and froze. A man was carrying a body over his shoulder, fireman-style, out to the back alley; a female by the looks of her long hair.

Mattie's heart sped up as thoughts whirled in her mind. *It was happening. Something was happening right now. How many victims had he snatched already? Were they dead or alive? How was she going to get her and Ren out of here without getting caught?* She glanced down the corridor to her left, to the way they had come in, but she couldn't see Ramsey or Jarek from where she was standing. And she was too afraid to move to grab their attention. *What if the man saw her?* She couldn't leave Ren unprotected. No way, no how. She was on her own for now.

"Dandy," she muttered through gritted teeth. "I hope Ren has to do Number Two."

The door squeaked open and Mattie whipped her head around. As the man moved closer, he passed under the dim light bulb near the men's bathroom. Mattie's heart dropped to her feet when she caught a glimpse of the person's face. *No, no, no,* her mind screamed. *It can't be true. It's impossible. How could this be?* It wasn't a dream, and her mind wasn't playing tricks on her. This was real and this person had to be stopped. *Now.*

Mattie imagined she would later wonder why her heart hadn't tried to beat itself out of her chest or her limbs hadn't turned into a quivering mass of Jell-O once this was all over. But she had to do something. And suddenly, all the training she'd had with Ty kicked in. She emptied her mind, took three deep breaths to slow her heart rate, hiked her dress up to above her knees, and shifted her weight to the balls of her feet.

The element of surprise was on her side and she was going to take full advantage. Of course, that was before the bathroom door opened. Then it was all instinct for Mattie. She pushed Ren as hard as she could. Momentarily distracted from her shriek of "Wha—? Hey!", Mattie's foot made a solid connection with the man's stomach. His breath whooshed out and he doubled over. She quickly followed with a sharp elbow jab to the back of his head, knocking him out cold.

"I believe your hosting days are over, Pepe," she murmured.

EPILOGUE

One month later

"It's been crazy around here the past few weeks. Sorry I haven't been by sooner. They almost cancelled the show, which was understandable after all that's happened. The night of the party, Pepe drugged and tried to kidnap four teenagers. Pepe isn't his real name, though. It's John-Michael Carsten. Hold on, it gets better. His father was the Director of the Starfire Foundation. I know that means nothing to you guys, but this place was the best bet for people in need of an organ donor."

It was a Saturday morning and Mattie was sprawled on her back under The Memory Tree, near her parents' crosses.

"Anyhow, Pepe...John-Michael...*whatever*, needed a lung transplant three years ago. Instead of waiting like everybody else, his father found a donor through the black market. Yeah, I know, rich people can be pretty twisted. During a lawsuit against a company his father used to work for, Pepe disappeared and popped up in Florida and then Los Angeles using two different names. His father was making him steal organs for his clients. Can you *believe* that? Want to know what's strangely freaky? That no matter where he went, or what job he found, Pepe-John was never at a loss for potential victims. He somehow managed to be in a position where he was surrounded by healthy teenagers. Yeah, I know. Freaky-deaky.

He was able to get his slimy hands on six teenagers before coming to Phoenix. And how he got that co-host job on DJP, I'll never know. What I *do* know is that he must've felt like he'd hit the jackpot being around all us kids. I can see him now, pointing his finger around the nightclub, saying 'eenie-meenie-

199

minie-moe, which one shall I knock out cold.' Crazy *haoli*."
Mattie sighed and shook her head.

"You know what sucks, though? He got six more kids
before he was stopped. Oh, not all of them lived here, but
still...you would've been proud of me, guys. For reals. I was
nervous and scared for Ren, but I finally got a chance to put all
that training to good use. Nice solid kick to the tum-tum and a
karate chop to the back of the head. I only knocked him out. I
wish I'd put him in a coma. But then again, if I had, he'd have
to wait to get better before going to jail. According to the news,
Pepe-John might get life without bail or parole. And his father
might get life or the death penalty. Notice I say might because
I'm being realistic here. It's not gonna happen. They're gonna
buy their way into a five-year-but-out-in-two-for-good-behavior
type of sentence. The man found his son a lung through the
black market, for Cripes sake. You don't think a person like that
has connections in the underworld? We're talkin' a little red
man with horns and a tail who lives in a very hot place.
Metaphorically speaking, of course, but you know what I
mean."

Mattie rolled over onto her stomach, propped herself up on
her elbows and waved her feet in the air. This was the way
Jarek found her moments later. Judah, who was keeping watch
nearby, raised his head in greeting, but didn't move from his
shady spot. Mattie had yet to notice his presence, because her
back was to him and she was still talking. So Jarek sat on the
tire swing and waited. And listened.

"Poor Sophie. Sophie Brown, that is. She was Pepe's co-
host on the show. She had no idea. No clue whatsoever. She
tried to keep it up by herself, but it wasn't the same. The hosting
gig, I mean. You could see it in her face. She was hounded by
reporters for days on end, accused of being in on the whole
scheme. She wasn't, of course. She was duped like the rest of

us. She left the show and moved away, I heard. I don't know if she's going to try to avoid testifying or what. I know *I* would. Who wants to be reminded that your best friend betrayed you?

It's a shame, really. Sophie and Pepe had this wonderful connection. On the show, they finished each other's sentences, played off each other's personalities. Something like that couldn't be scripted, y'know? We all thought they were a couple. There was speculation, y'know, but no one knew for sure. I suppose it's a moot point now. Instead of finding new people, the producers decided to let the regulars host the show," Mattie paused to laugh.

"I have to say that I was nervous talking on national television for the first time. It's different than the dancing, y'know? Dancing is something I do anyway, something I'm used to. But we all take turns, and having Jarek there is a major plus." Mattie stopped, looked down and absently plucked blades of grass. "You'd like him. Jarek, I mean. He reminds me of you, Kel. And Ty. In some ways. He's honorable, kind, funny, doesn't mind that I can kick his butt any day of the week, absolutely gorgeous, positively beautiful, and an exceptional kisser—"

Mattie stopped abruptly and slapped a hand over her mouth. She closed her eyes and shook her head.

"I can't believe I just said that," she mumbled. "I wouldn't even say that to Ty."

Jarek bit his lip to keep from laughing aloud.

Mattie waved a frantic hand in the air. "Okay, so, forget that last part. It was TMI for you anyway and you're probably going to get a small kine huhu, but it's all minors. Really. The thing is... I love him. And I trust him. It's been so hard for me to do that, y'know? But being on the show and being with Jarek has made me see that I can't close a part of myself off forever. I don't want to be like Pepe, trying to get away from my past. I need to confront it and move on. Which is what I'm doing today. I've decided to tell Mici and Ren. I know, I know, I should've told them sooner. Well, years ago, in fact, but better late than never, yeah? So...wish me luck. I love you guys. We'll talk again soon."

Mattie kissed her fingertips then pressed them on each of the five crosses. She sat back on her knees and stared into space for a moment.

"So what exactly is a small kine huhu?"

The unexpected male voice made Mattie yelp in surprise. She was on her feet in an instant, crouched low in the ready fighting stance, weight shifted to the balls of her feet. At the sight of Jarek sitting in her tire swing, elbows propped on his knees, she slowly straightened. Casting an accusing glare at Judah, who purposely ignored her she was sure, Mattie propped a hand on her outthrust hip.

"How long have you been there?" she demanded.

Jarek smiled and stood up. "Not long," he lied.

As he walked towards her, Mattie took in the plain white T-shirt that strained across his chest, the jeans encasing his long legs, and his bare feet. Sunglasses rested on top of his head, holding back the silky fall of hair he was starting to wear down more often. Mattie knew he was doing it for her, because she loved running her fingers through it. Hair back or hair down, it didn't matter, for he was quickly becoming a favorite with the ladies. His best friend, Gunner, too. Mattie couldn't be jealous because she was garnering her fair share of attention as well.

She smiled, thinking of the way he always stuck close to her side as they left the club every Friday and Saturday night, signing autographs and taking pictures. Never mind that she could beat them all off with a stick. Literally. But Mattie loved being near him, so she let him believe he was protecting her. And Jarek loved her, so he was glad that she allowed it.

Stopping in front of her, he cupped her face in his hands and leaned down to brush his lips softly against hers. Angling his head in the other direction, Jarek deepened the kiss, enfolding her close to his chest. What seemed like an eternity later, Jarek sprinkled little nibbling pecks on her forehead, both cheeks and her chin before leaning back to look down at her.

"Hey, Blue Eyes," he greeted in a low tone, smiling.

"Hey, beautiful," Mattie said.

Jarek could feel the blush steeling over his face even as his smile grew wider. He was still getting used to the endearment, but he loved hearing it.

Mattie laughed and stood on tiptoe to lay a smacking kiss on both red cheeks.

"So, you never did tell me. What does small kine huhu mean?" Jarek wanted to know.

"It's Hawaiian slang for a little bit angry," Mattie told him.

Jarek nodded once. "Uh-huh. And the minors thing? I'm guessing you weren't talking baseball."

Mattie laughed again and shook her head. "No big deal."

"So? Tell me, anyway."

Mattie sighed and rolled her eyes. "I just did, goofball. It means no big deal."

"More Hawaiian slang?"

"More Hawaiian slang."

Jarek nodded again. "You're going to have to keep me updated on stuff like that. I came to get you. The girls are here. Are you ready?" he asked, giving her a tight hug.

Mattie hugged him back then smiled into his eyes. "I'm ready."

COMING SOON!

Mataya's guardian, Tykota Black Hawk, will soon have someone new to watch over. Keep an eye out for the:

DRAVEN ATREIDES, TEENAGE INFORMANT SERIES

ABOUT THE AUTHOR

Celise Downs was born and currently lives in Arizona. She shares her home with her husband and a talkative Tabby cat named Sweet Pea. When she's not writing, she enjoys reading, going to the movies, and watching her favorite television shows.

Celise loves to hear from readers who enjoyed her books, so be sure to drop her a line at www.celisedowns.com.

LaVergne, TN USA
29 July 2010
191396LV00007B/86/P